P9-EKY-546

HERGÉ
★
THE ADVENTURES OF
TINTIN
★
THE
BLACK
ISLAND

EGMONT

TRANSLATED BY LESLIE LONSDALE-COOPER AND MICHAEL TURNER

EGMONT
We bring stories to life

The Black Island
Artwork copyright © 1956, 1984 by Editions Casterman, Paris and Tournai.
Text copyright © 1975 Egmont UK Limited.

King Ottokar's Sceptre
Artwork copyright © 1947, 1975 by Editions Casterman, Paris and Tournai.
Text copyright © 1958 Egmont UK Limited.

The Crab with the Golden Claws
Artwork copyright © 1953, 1981 by Editions Casterman, Paris and Tournai.
Text copyright © 1958 Egmont UK Limited.

First published in this edition 2015 by Egmont UK Limited
The Yellow Building, 1 Nicholas Road, London W11 4AN

ISBN 978 1 4052 8277 2

64056/1

Printed in China

THE BLACK ISLAND

A plane in trouble?

RRRR

PFTT
PFTT

PFTT

PFTT

PFTT

Sounds bad.

It's probably a private aircraft.

Let's see, Snowy.

Will it take long to fix?

No, only a few minutes. Nothing seriously wrong.

Why, it's an unregistered plane.

Someone coming, Mick.

Too bad for him! You know our orders.

Are you in trouble? Can I help?

Next morning . . .

Well, doctor?

He was lucky. The bullet only grazed a rib. He'll be up and about in a couple of days.

Excuse me, nurse.

Can we see Tintin, please?

You can go in.

Look here: are you absolutely sure the plane had no registration marks?

Quite certain.

It all looks very fishy to me.

To be precise: the whole thing looks like me, very fishy.

Telephone, please, for Mr Thomson or Mr Thompson.

Hello? . . . Yes . . . Interpol? . . . Yes sir, Thompson, with a p, as in psychology . . . From Scotland Yard? . . . Eastdown? Last night? . . . Yes sir, I understand. We'll leave at once.

We're going back to England. An unregistered plane crashed last night near a place called Eastdown, in Sussex. Goodbye.

Goodbye, and watch your step!

Thanks!

CRASH

?

Why can't you look where you're going?

To be precise: speak for yourself.

Eastdown . . . If only . . . It can't be helped, I simply must go. Never mind doctor's orders!

Goodbye, nurse. Many thanks!

Ach! The silly fools! Who d'you think they shot at last night? Tintin himself!

Pity they didn't finish him off while they were about it.

Look!!

KÖLN
BRUXELLES
LONDON

Why have we stopped?

Let's look in the corridor.

There's a door open, and someone's getting out. Come on, Snowy!

There he goes!

What d'you think you're doing?

Eek!

Let me go! A man just jumped off the train. We must follow him!

You can't fool me.

Everybody stay where you are!

No one is to leave the train.

He's coming round.

Tintin! Aren't you in bed?

There he is! I'd know him anywhere. He knocked me out!

Me??

Aha! A cosh! Useful for knocking people on the head.

!

Robbery, too! Here's the poor man's wallet, in your other pocket.

!?

I'm innocent, I tell you! It's a trick. Someone planted the cosh and the wallet in my pockets while I was asleep . . . I've never seen them before.

What else can we do Tintin? The evidence is all against you.

I agree.

It's true. Everything points to my guilt. And the guard can swear I was trying to get away. Very neatly planned. But why? And by whom?

?

The key to the handcuffs! Well done, Snowy. Bring it here!

ZZZZ

ZZZ

Good gracious, we've stopped ... Good heavens, where's Tintin?

I ... er ... don't know.

He's given us the slip. Got away, with handcuffs, too. What a cheek! . . .

To be precise: he's given us away. Slipped us the handcuffs, too. What a sneak! . . .

6

An hour later . . .

Good! A village. Perhaps I can hire a car to take me to the coast.

CLINK CLINK CLINK

Just wait till I get my hands on him!

To be precise: . . . er . . . just wait till we get our hands!

Hello!

Tintin!

!

You!

Hey, stop!

That's what they call putting your head in the lion's mouth!

Stop him! Stop him!

Where's he gone?

Excuse me, sir. Have you seen a young man running past your house?

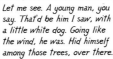

Let me see. A young man, you say. That'd be him I saw, with a little white dog. Going like the wind, he was. Hid himself among those trees, over there.

Aha! We've got him!

Snowy!

WOOAH WOOAH

!

Snowy's given the game away!

It's Tintin!

Stop! You're under arrest!

We're gaining on him!

To be precise: we're . . .

It's your own fault. If you'd kept quiet, none of this would have happened.

Here comes a lorry, going our way. I'll try to thumb a ride.

Lucky for me you're going right to the docks. I'm trying to catch the cross-channel ferry. Think we'll make it?

All right! Haul off the gangway!

So, my friend, we are safely away. Our little plan was a good one, eh?

Not bad at all! By the time Tintin has finished proving his innocence we shall be well clear . . .

WHEW!

8

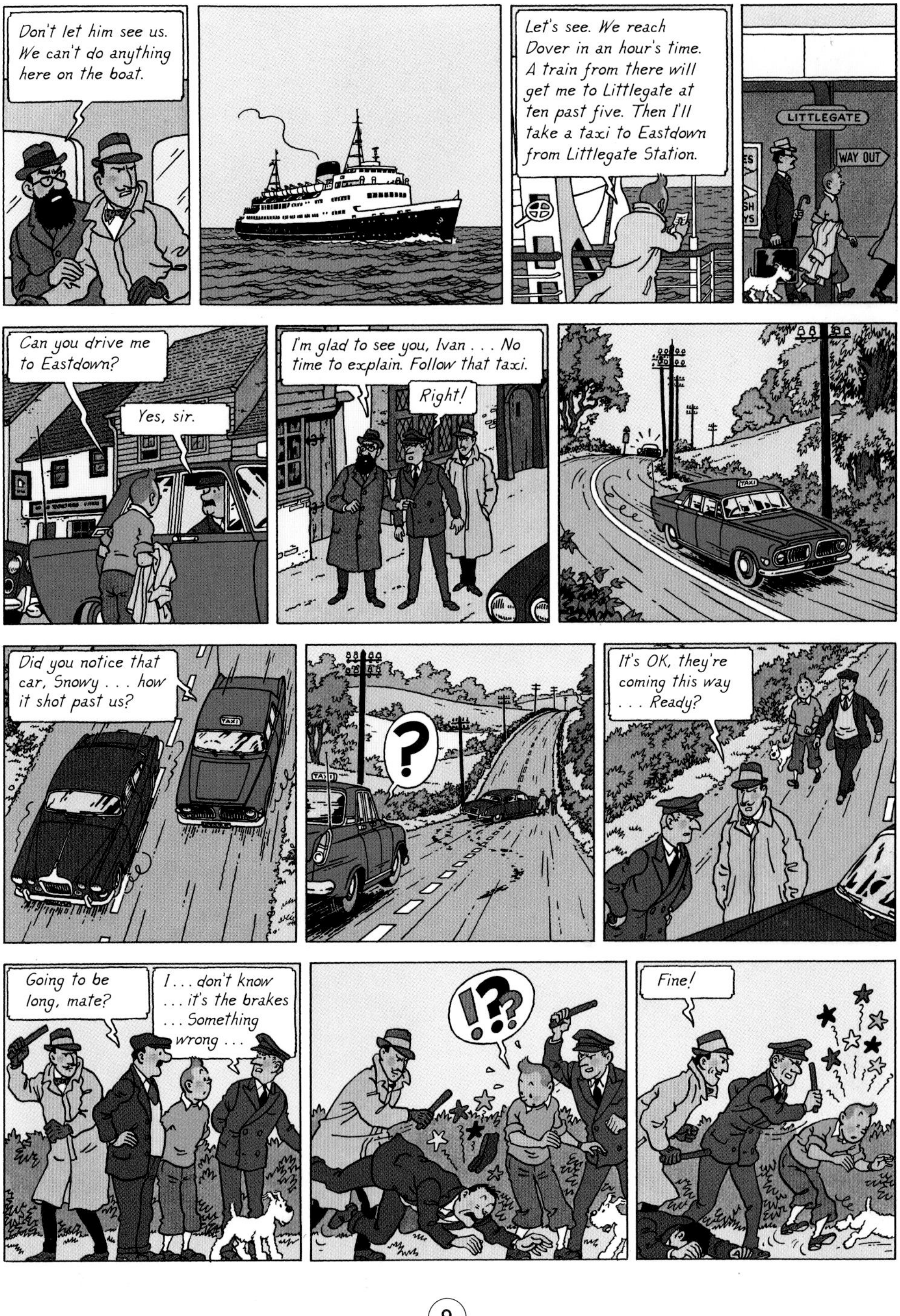

Don't let him see us. We can't do anything here on the boat.
Let's see. We reach Dover in an hour's time. A train from there will get me to Littlegate at ten past five. Then I'll take a taxi to Eastdown from Littlegate Station.
LITTLEGATE
WAY OUT
Can you drive me to Eastdown?
Yes, sir.
I'm glad to see you, Ivan . . . No time to explain. Follow that taxi.
Right!
TAXI
Did you notice that car, Snowy . . . how it shot past us?
TAXI
TAXI
?
It's OK, they're coming this way . . . Ready?
Going to be long, mate?
I . . . don't know . . . it's the brakes . . . Something wrong . . .
!??
Fine!

Too easy!

Look, Puschov; our friend Tintin is coming round.

Aha!

So, you managed to escape from the police. It would have been wiser to stay safely behind bars.

Stop, Ivan. This will do.

OK.

Get out! And don't try to be clever with me!

Don't you think this joke has gone far enough? What do you want with me?

You needn't put on an act for us. You know as well as we do.

Undo the rope.

Good. Now, my brilliant friend, you are going to become the world high-diving champion. Jump!

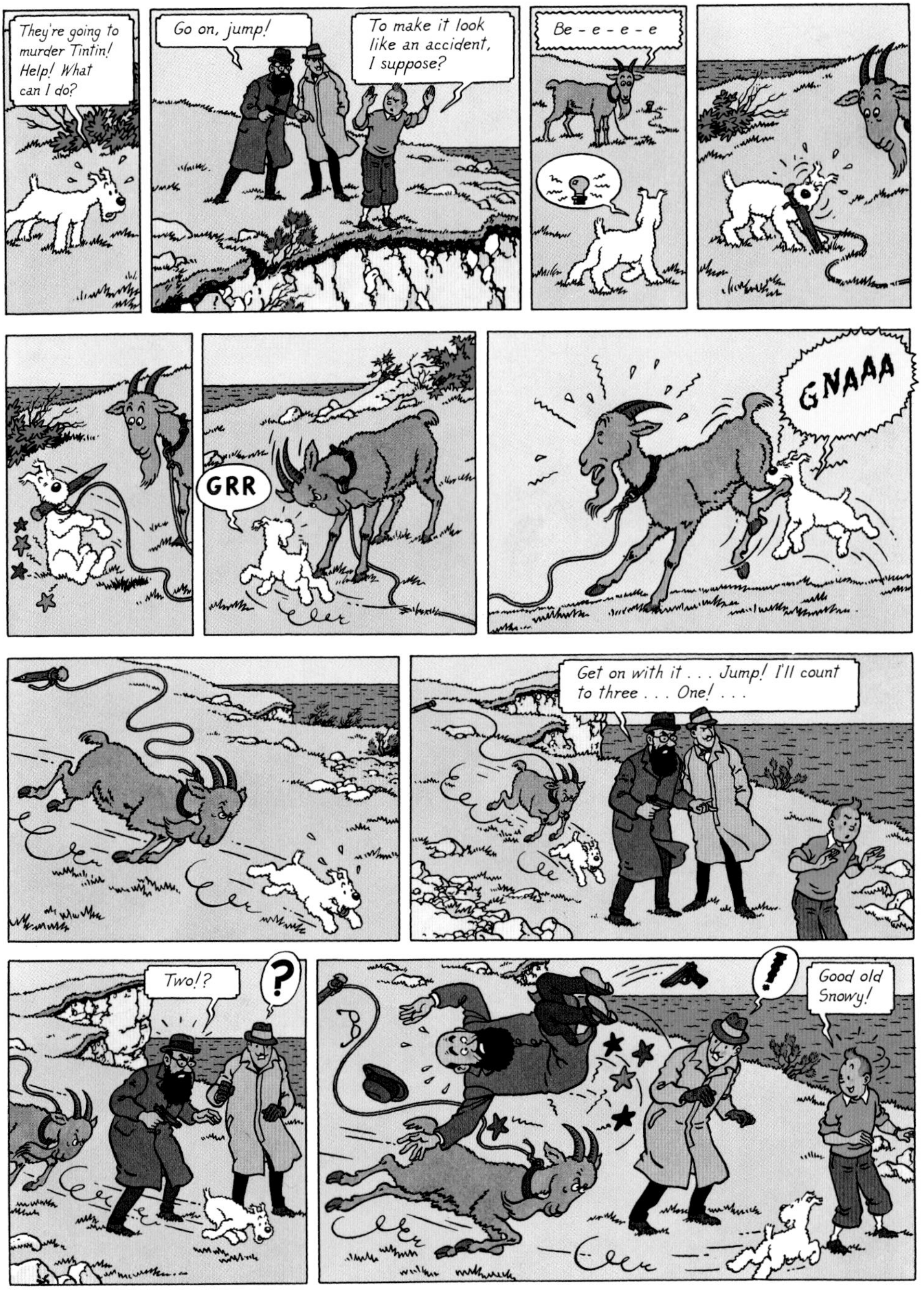
They're going to murder Tintin! Help! What can I do?
Go on, jump!
To make it look like an accident, I suppose?
Be - e - e - e
GRR
GNAAA
Get on with it . . . Jump! I'll count to three . . . One! . . .
Two!?
?
!
Good old Snowy!

All right . . .
Hands up!

Look out! They're
coming back!

Let's get out of here!

Don't worry, we'll make
sure of him next time.

Come on, Snowy,
we must get
moving.

You have some brilliant
ideas, Snowy. But don't
let them run away
with you!

Hello . . . Ja . . . Doctor Müller
speaking . . . So, it is you . . .
What? . . . Tintin on our trail
. . . Kruzitürcken! We shall
have to keep our eyes open.

Hello, the wreckage of the plane that crashed last night. Come on, let's have a look.

What a mess. What happened to the pilot?

Don't know, sir. We found this lot this morning. No sign of the crew. They must have baled out when they ran into trouble.

It's the plane I saw yesterday. Definitely. But I shan't learn much from this pile of scrap-metal.

Snowy!

Snowy's on to something!

He's picked up a scent; it must be the crew.

There isn't a dog in the world like him. He can smell out a crook a mile away.

Better be on our guard; we must be getting close.

Careful . . . Mustn't take any risks.

Here we go! He's found something.

Aren't you ashamed, wasting our time bone-hunting. Here, give it to me.

I've told you dozens of times, you're not to chew filthy old bones.

Here, Snowy! Come here at once!

WOOAH

WOOAH! WOOAH!

!?

Strange . . . He really does want me to follow him.

I'll come. But woe betide you if it's just another bone.

?

Flying jackets! Those thugs from the plane must have hidden them.

Too much to hope they'd leave anything in the pockets.

Aha! Look there! Some scraps of paper. Something's been torn up. Perhaps this will give us a lead.

I've always liked puzzles, and this time I've got a real one!

That's done it.

Hmm. Not much help. What on earth can it mean? . . .

Oh, Snowy, not again!

. . . and let that be an end of bones for today!

OUCH!

Can't you look what you're doing? . . . Anyway, you're trespassing; this is private property.

I'm sorry. I didn't know. I lost my way . . .

All right, this time. But don't let me catch you again. Take the path down to the river, cross the bridge, and you'll see the main road.

Snowy! Are you trying to make a fool of me?

There's the road.

It must be a couple of miles to Eastdown.

Dr J.W.MÜLLER

No one about. I'll take a look around.

WOOF WOOF

WOOF! WOOF!

I'm done for!

WOOF! WOOF!

WOOF!! WOOF!!

WOOF!! WOOF!!

Snowy! Snowy! He'll be eaten alive!

WOOF!

WOO-OO-OAH!

GRRR

Here, Snowy! Come here!

We must get out. The dog may have raised the alarm.

YEOW!

A man-trap!

RRRING

Ach so! Someone is caught in trap number nine. Let us take a look.

What a pleasant surprise! Tintin himself, come specially to see me.

Release him, Ivan. He won't run.

Get the car out. We're leaving at once.

It was a mistake to meddle in our affairs. I shall now have to dispose of you. Fortunately, I happen to be medical superintendent of a private mental institution: rather a special institution. Not all of my patients are insane when they are admitted . . .

. . . but after eight hours of . . . special treatment, they are unlikely to recover. Excuse me: I must make a telephone call then I shall be entirely at your service.

I wonder . . .

Hello, Horncliffe? . . . I have a young patient for you . . . highly . . . er . . . dangerous. He will require treatment B . . . You understand? Good!

. . . a burning log?

Got one . . . hold it against the rope . . .

As usual, he seems entirely sane, but . . . after the treatment . . . you follow me?

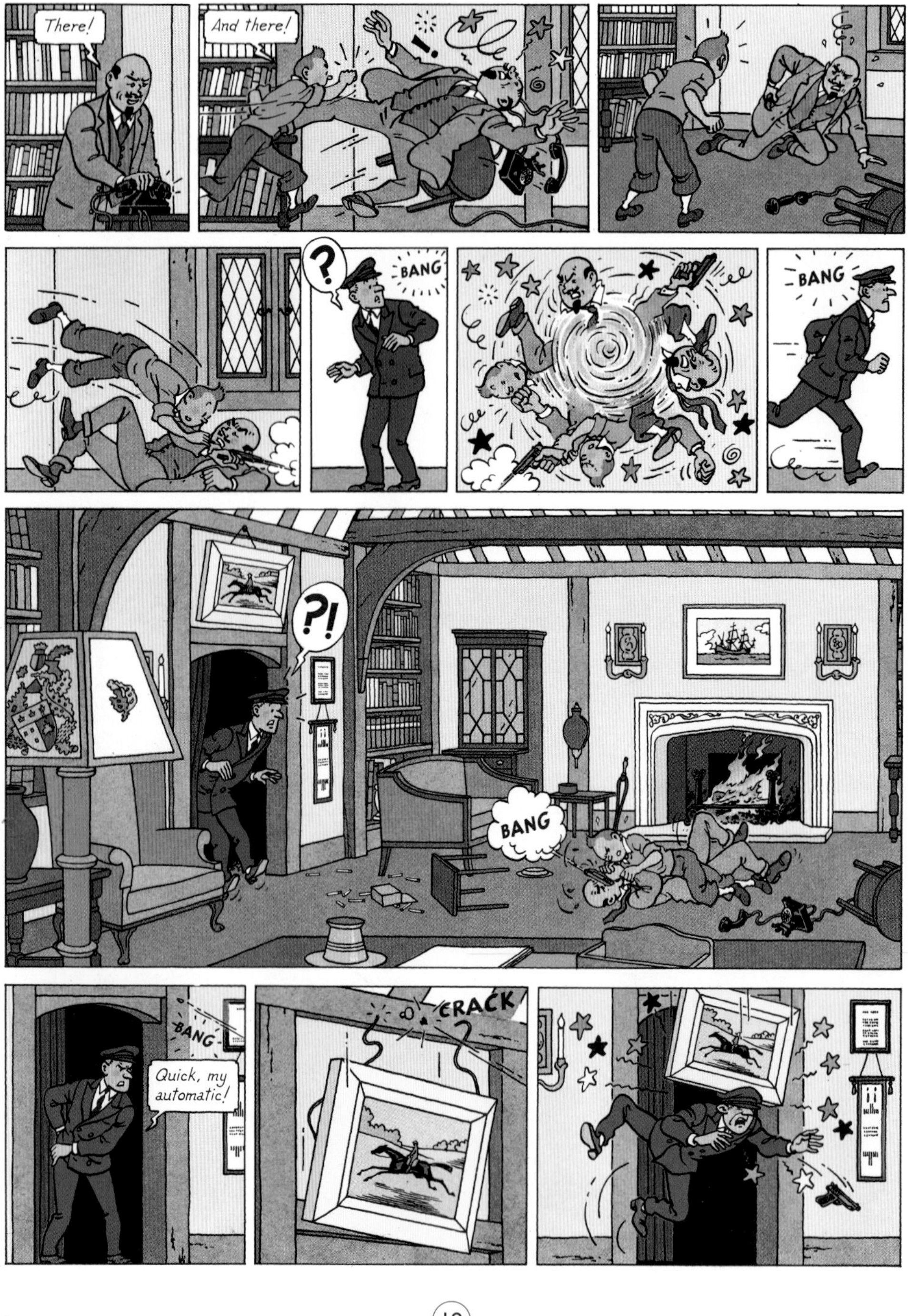
There!
And there!
BANG
BANG
?!
BANG
BANG
Quick, my automatic!
CRACK

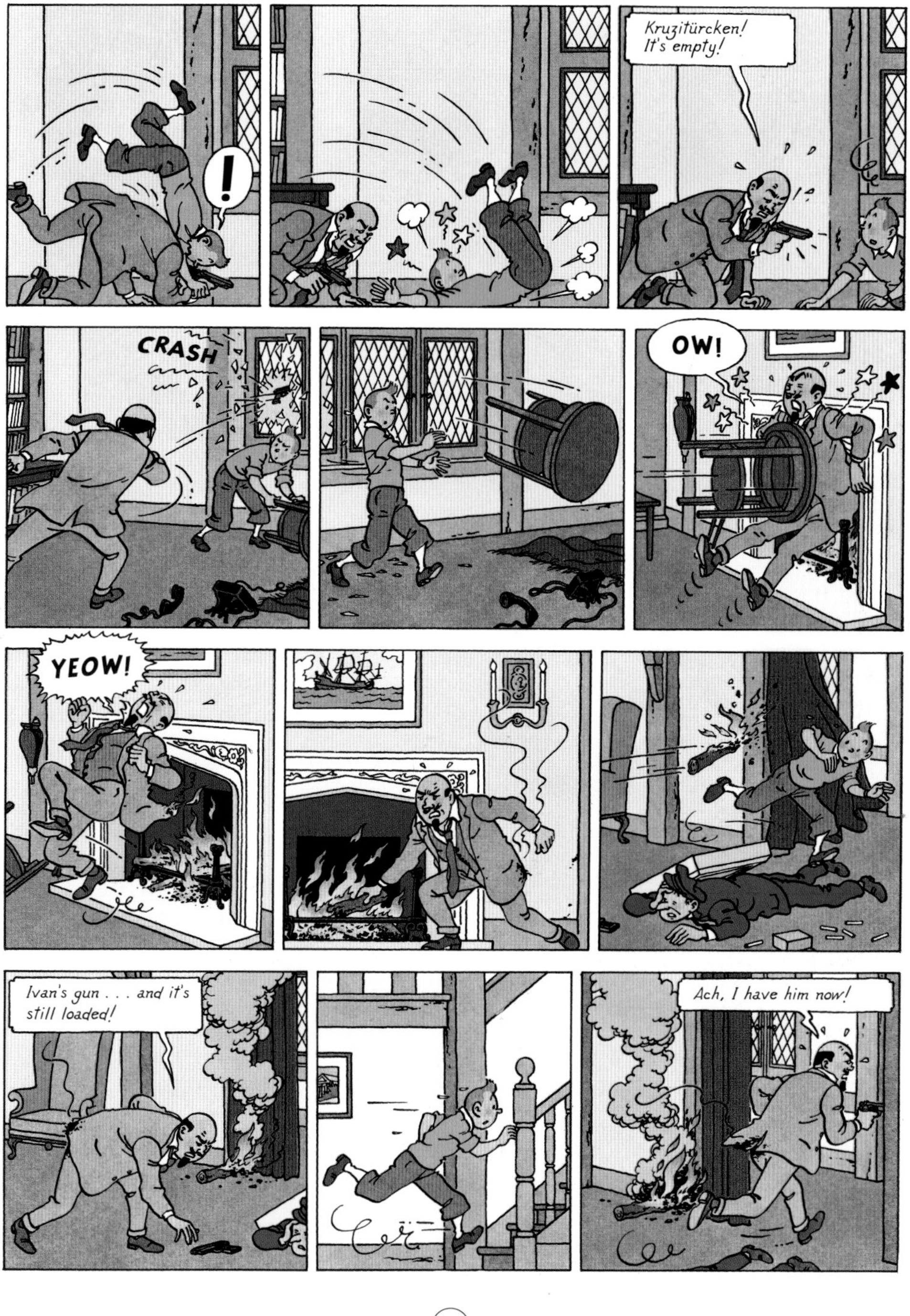
!
Kruzitürcken! It's empty!
CRASH
OW!
YEOW!
Ivan's gun . . . and it's still loaded!
Ach, I have him now!

THUD

BANG   BANG

ZZINGG

CHLOROFORM

FIRE! FIRE!

?

!

FIRE! FIRE!

Himmel! That burning log I threw: it set the room alight!

Fire? Is it a real alarm, or just a trick to make me open the door?

What's the matter? I feel dead tired . . . Come on, this is no time to fall asleep . . . I simply must . . .

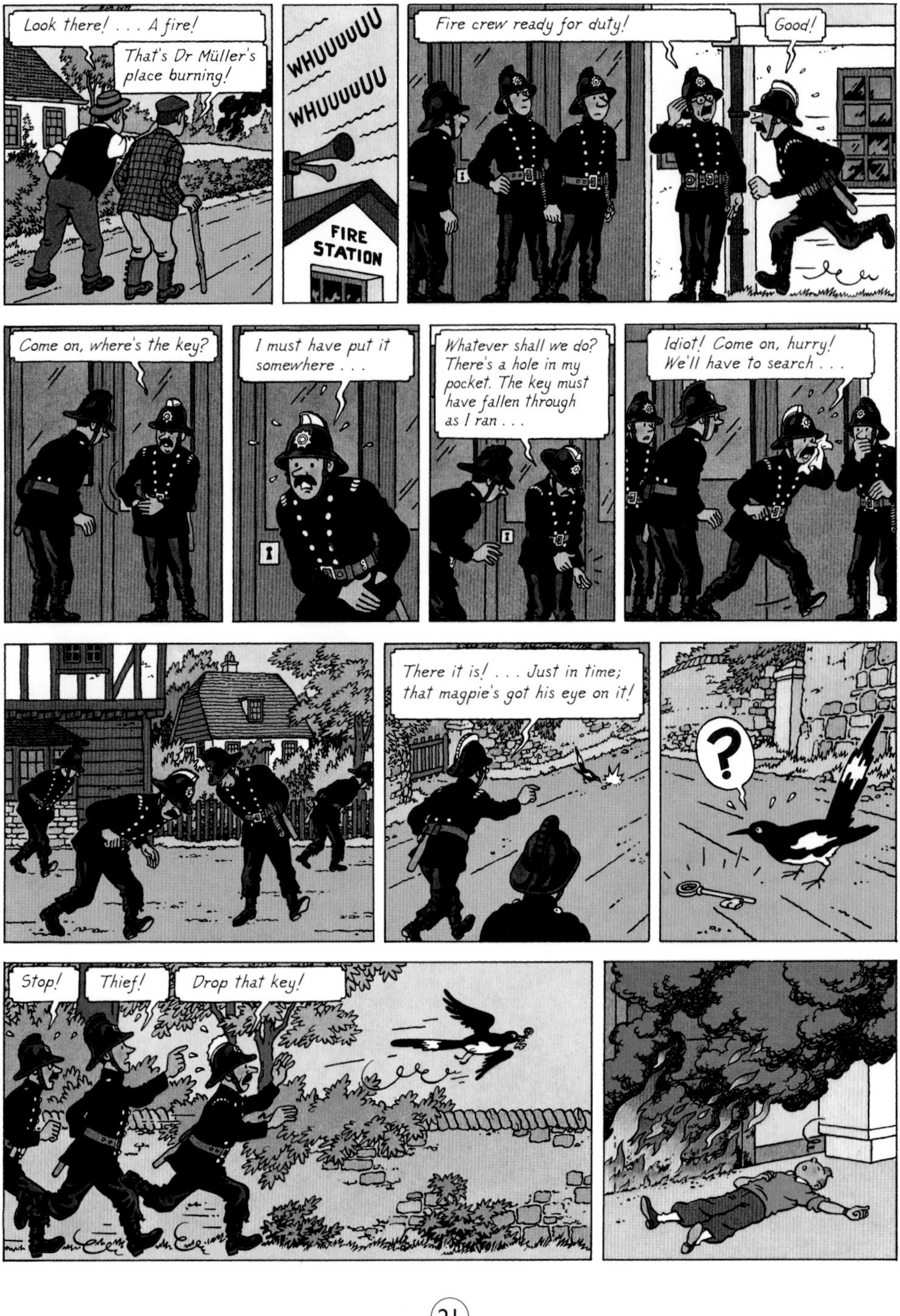
Look there! . . . A fire!
That's Dr Müller's place burning!
WHUUUUUU
WHUUUUUU
FIRE STATION
Fire crew ready for duty!
Good!
Come on, where's the key?
I must have put it somewhere . . .
Whatever shall we do? There's a hole in my pocket. The key must have fallen through as I ran . . .
Idiot! Come on, hurry! We'll have to search . . .
There it is! . . . Just in time; that magpie's got his eye on it!
?
Stop!
Thief!
Drop that key!

Got it!

AAH!

AAAH!

Open the door, quick!

All right . . . just a minute . . . I . . .

Goodness gracious! I've mixed them up. This isn't the key to the station!

So there you are, Fred. How many times have I told you, that's the key to my jam cupboard!

DING DING DING

What accursed luck! The fire brigade!

Anyone left inside the house, Doctor?

Fortunately not. We all escaped.

Wooah! Wooah! They must save Tintin! How can I make them understand? Wooah!

I must stop them at all costs, or they'll find him!

They're busy . . . now for it . . . no-one will notice me.

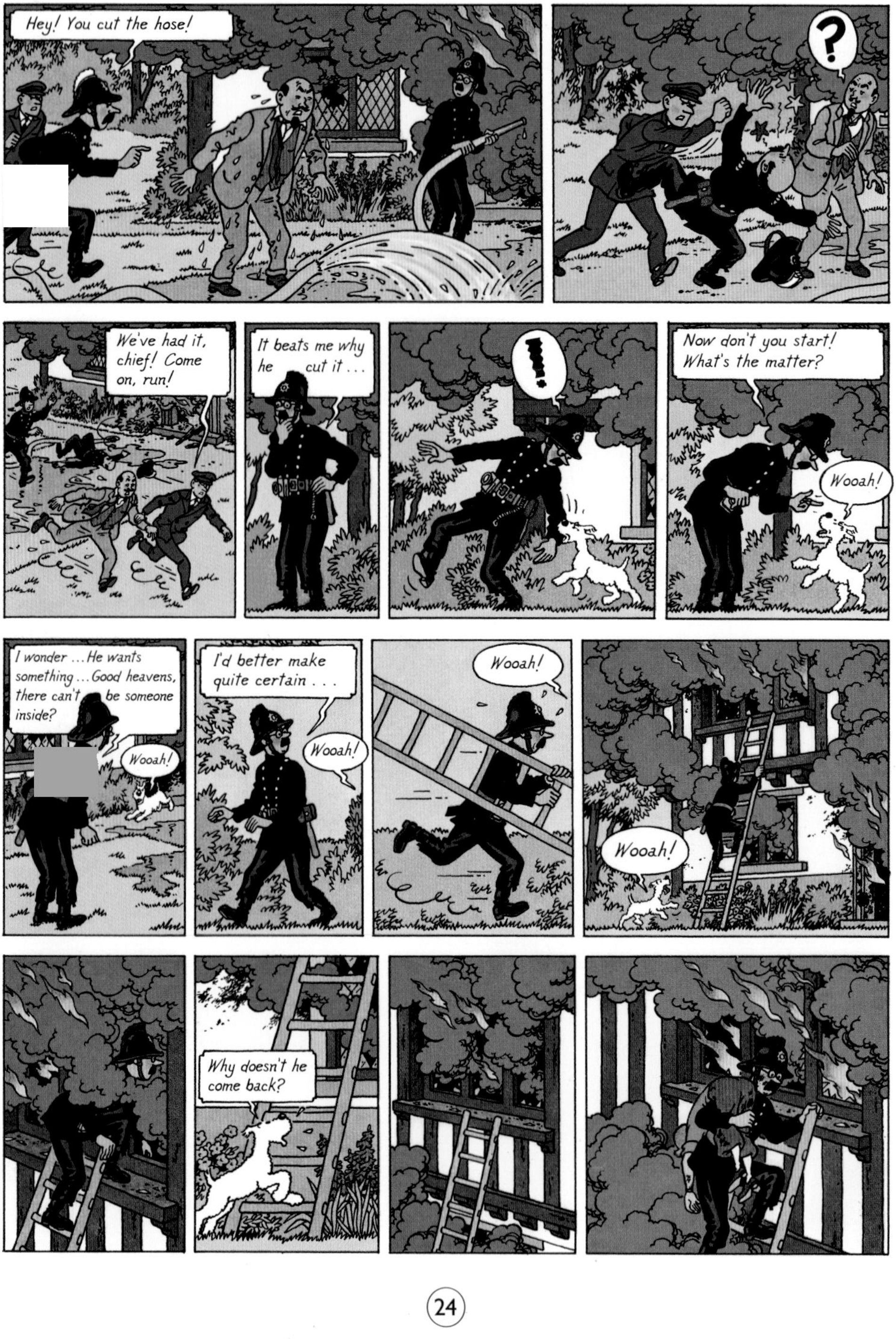
Hey! You cut the hose!
We've had it, chief! Come on, run!
It beats me why he cut it . . .
Now don't you start! What's the matter?
Wooah!
I wonder ... He wants something ... Good heavens, there can't be someone inside?
Wooah!
I'd better make quite certain . . .
Wooah!
Wooah!
Wooah!
Why doesn't he come back?

Next morning...

...And what happened to Doctor Müller?

I'm afraid my men couldn't catch him. His car was standing just by the house. He hopped in, with his driver, and they went off at top speed. We hadn't a chance.

A pity. I'd give a lot to know... why were they so anxious to get rid of me? Never mind. Perhaps I'll find a clue at the house, to put me on their track again... The fire can't have destroyed everything...

You're not getting out of bed?

Of course. I feel absolutely all right.

Heavens! There isn't much left of Dr Müller's house: it's gutted.

I shan't find anything useful here...

?

Electric cables. What can they be for?

They seem to go on...

How odd. Where on earth can they lead?

?

CRACK

?

A red beacon. I don't understand . . .

That isn't all. The wires continue along here.

I say, Tintin, are you going to do this all day?

There's another light here, too.

And now a third one . . .

The three trees are connected in a triangle . . .

GOT IT!

These are instructions to the pilot in that plane. 3 f. r. △ means three flares, red, in a triangle. A signal!

Meanwhile . . .

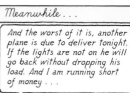

And the worst of it is, another plane is due to deliver tonight. If the lights are not on he will go back without dropping his load. And I am running short of money . . .

We must return, Ivan. This is the plan. We enter the grounds after dark and light the beacons; the plane drops its load, which we put into the car. By tomorrow morning we can be out of the country. What do you think?

Good idea, chief.

That night . . .

Himmel! The cables have been pulled up. Someone has discovered our installation.

Look over there, chief. The beacons are alight!

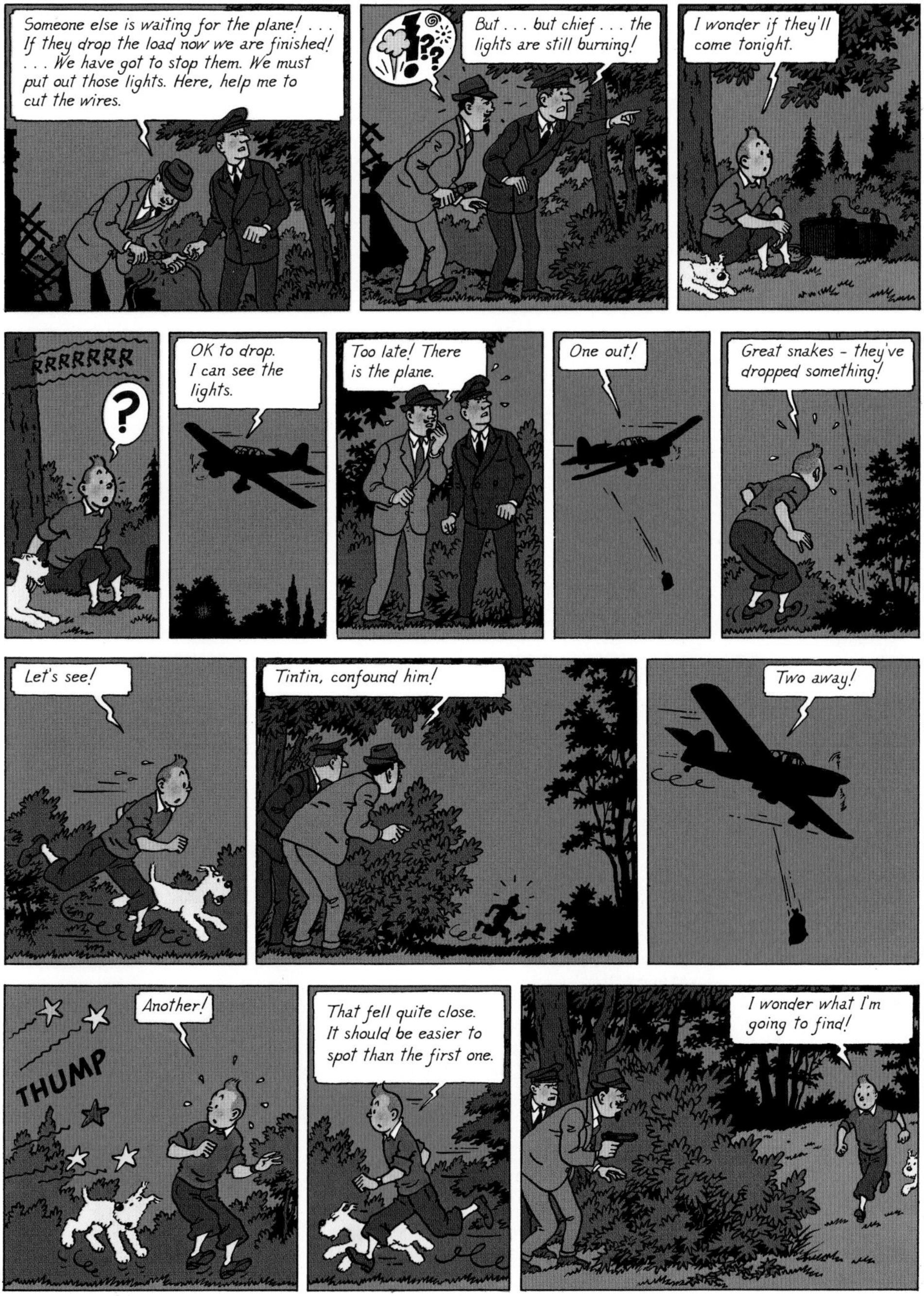
Someone else is waiting for the plane! . . . If they drop the load now we are finished! . . . We have got to stop them. We must put out those lights. Here, help me to cut the wires.
But . . . but chief . . . the lights are still burning!
I wonder if they'll come tonight.
RRRRRRR
?
OK to drop. I can see the lights.
Too late! There is the plane.
One out!
Great snakes - they've dropped something!
Let's see!
Tintin, confound him!
Two away!
Another!
THUMP
That fell quite close. It should be easier to spot than the first one.
I wonder what I'm going to find!

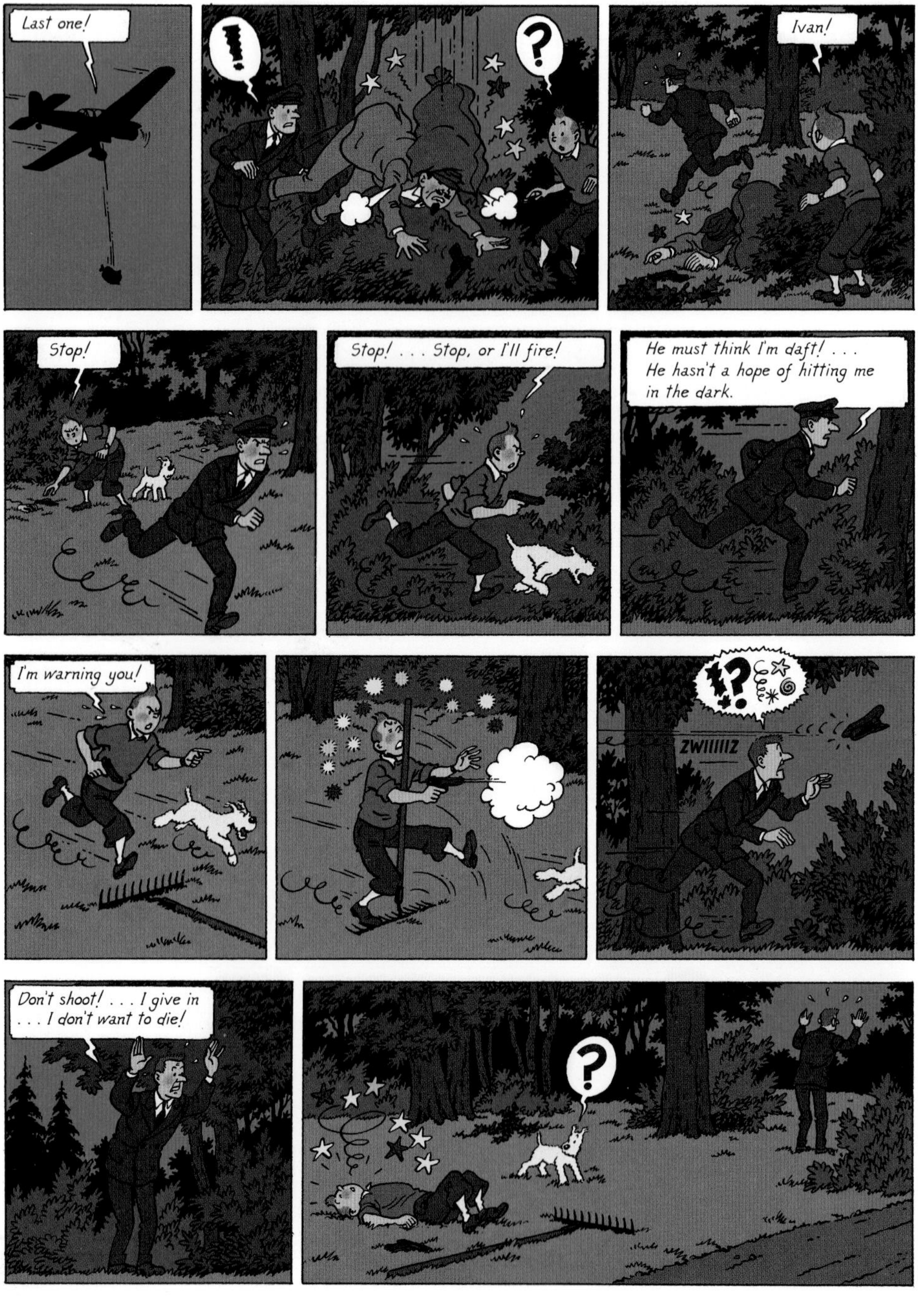
Last one!
!
?
Ivan!
Stop!
Stop! . . . Stop, or I'll fire!
He must think I'm daft! . . . He hasn't a hope of hitting me in the dark.
I'm warning you!
!?
ZWIIIIIZ
Don't shoot! . . . I give in . . . I don't want to die!
?

Can I put my hands down now? I won't play any tricks.

Wake up, Tintin!

?

OHO!

Stupid fool! He trod on the rake and knocked himself out. I'll just take his gun . . .

Golly, what can I do?

WHAK

Quits!

Out cold!

The most important thing is to truss them up securely!

Necessity is the mother of invention, so they say. If you haven't any rope, use wire . . .

Now for the sacks. Let's see what they contain . . .

Great snakes! Banknotes!

Forgers! So that's your game. You'll go to gaol for this!

I'd better set about finding the other two sacks.

There's one . . .

?

EEK!

OWW!

They're getting away!

I'm an idiot! When they struggled, they caused a short-circuit, and the wires burned.

Hurry!

The car! They're getting away. Not a hope of stopping them . . . Unless . . .

It's my only chance . . . If they come this way, it's still possible . . .

He'll break his neck!

Aha! . . .

Steady now . . . I must time it precisely . . .

Whoops!

Why couldn't he use the gate, like me? . . . He always enjoys pretending to be an acrobat . . . Some people never learn!

To let them get away like that – right under my very nose!

Under his nose! They very nearly went over it!

A car! I'll stop it!

PARP
PAARP

There's a car just ahead . . . crooks making a getaway . . . I simply must go after them . . .

Crooks? . . . I say, what a lark! . . . Hop in the caravan.

We aren't exactly beating the land-speed record! We'll catch them . . . provided they have a puncture!

The old girl's a bit sluggish; we'll be OK when she warms up.

Didn't I say so? . . . Better already!

Now we're for it!

SPLOSH

Now then, I'm booking you for camping on private property . . . And in the second place, you've been picking unauthorised fruit . . . And the third offence, swimming in a manner liable to cause a breach of the peace!

NO BATHING

Oh well, there's no hope of catching them now.

Look, a smash.

Great snakes! It's their car! . . . Will you drop me here, please?

The occupants? . . . Not a scratch. I saw them go off towards the railway station . . .

They're going to catch that train!

The train's pulling out!

He'll go flat on his face again! Just watch!

Come on, Snowy!

I made it - this time!

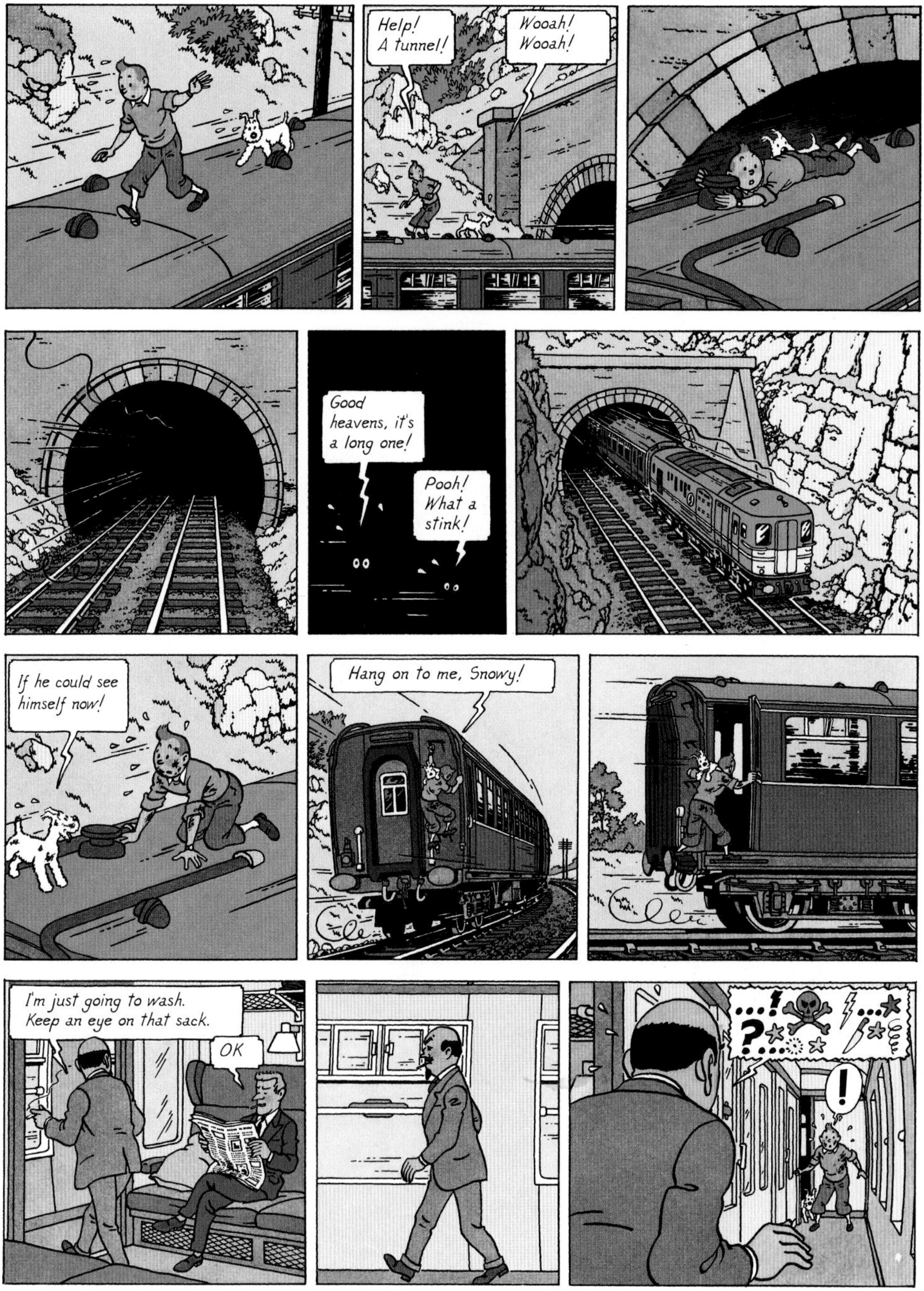
Help! A tunnel!
Wooah! Wooah!
Good heavens, it's a long one!
Pooh! What a stink!
If he could see himself now!
Hang on to me, Snowy!
I'm just going to wash. Keep an eye on that sack.
OK
!

Stop!

Stop him!

What's going on?

Now then, young man...

Let me get past...

Get out of here! Tintin's on the train!

?

More delay! All those questions; they'd have kept me talking all day ... There isn't a moment to lose ...

No time to be polite!

A little chicken for you, madam?

Ah!

Sorry!

!

!

Right?

Yes, yes, I've almost finished.

10 20

38

34

Hey, what's going on? The train's pulling up.

That's it. The automatic brake will soon stop the coaches.

Bravo!

They've got away . . . cunning devils!

Can't say I'm sorry. Now I can enjoy my dinner in peace.

Come on, Snowy, we've no time to hang around. It may be hours before a relief engine arrives.

♪

Look, Snowy, we're in luck! There's a goods train just moving off.

Hup!

LOCH LOMON
WHISKY

Oops!

Long time since this was an egg!

LOCH LOMOND
WHISKY

Hello, it's raining.

Golly, that's not water! But it's got a certain something, all the same!

Aha! There must be a leak . . .

Better try to clean myself up.

STOP!

A station? . . . No . . . Then I wonder why they've stopped.

What in the world . . . ? An engine, just sitting there . . .

It's the one they hijacked. Müller must have abandoned it . . . But where did they go? The driver may give me a lead . . .

Bert! Are you all right? What happened?

A couple of thugs . . . climbed into the cab . . . made us drive on . . . then ordered me to stop. One of 'em got behind us, clobbered me with a spanner . . . I went out like a light. Didn't see which way they went . . .

That's all right. My dog will pick up their trail in a flash . . . . Snowy!

Now where's he gone? . . . Snowy! . . . Hey, Snowy!

SNOWY!

S'OK, I'm c-c-coming . . . Give . . . hic . . . give a dog a sh-sh-shance . . .

Good heavens, he's tight!

Jush . . . hic . . . jush look what I can . . . do!

You ought to be ashamed of yourself! . . . Disgusting! . . . You're worse than a mongrel from the gutter!

Now pull yourself together, and pick up the scent. We're chasing gangsters . . . remember?

It's not . . . hic . . . fair . . . Hic . . . Two of you . . . picking on a . . . hic . . . poor little dog! . . .

Ah, a pub . . . and Snowy's got wind of something!

Wooah!

He's after them! He never really lets me down.

Wooah!

Wooah! Wooah!

LOCH LOMOND WHISKY

If you don't watch out you'll come to a sticky end!

LOMOND ISKY

Himmel! | So we meet again, eh?

Great snakes! | What?

You won't get away this time!

Whoa there! Not so fast!

Let me go! . . . Don't you understand? . . . They're thugs, gangsters . . . They'll escape!

We know your little tricks!

How did he manage to get here so soon?

WHITE HART

It's absurd . . . they're crooks, I tell you . . . and you're letting them get away.

So you say. In the meantime we're arresting you . . . The robbery on the train: or have you forgotten that little episode?

It's ridiculous! You're not still flogging that dead horse? . . . Look here, let's make a deal. Don't arrest me till those thugs are behind bars, then I'll give myself up.

Hmm! . . . What do you think?

Hmm! . . . It's . . . er . . . highly irregular . . . But on second thoughts, we might . . . er . . . stretch a point.

All right, we agree. We'll let you go, on one condition: we come with you.

Two minds with one thought, eh? If he pulls something off, we get all the credit.

Keep it up, Snowy!

I only hope we're not too late!

HALCHESTER
FLYING
CLUB

PARKING

Look! Over there! That plane taking off . . . I bet it's them!

Watch out! He's diving at us!

G-AREI

Ruffians!

To be precise: road-hogs!

Our hats . . . ?

There.

The vandals! Our best hats, almost brand new . . . a pair of perfect bowlers!

I remember when we bought them, seven years ago . . . A bowl of perfect purlers!

I'm beginning to agree with Tintin: they look like crooks.

To be precise: so do I. Tintin may be right: they cook like rooks!

RRRR

? ?

Wait for me, I'll be back! Goodbye!

Come on! After them! That other machine over there . . . Quick!

We're police officers . . . Start her up . . . We're taking off right away!

But sir, I . . .

That's enough! No ifs or buts! We're the police, see? And we're commandeering this plane, and you to fly it!

Police . . . Understand?

Full throttle, pilot!

You can cut out the . . . er . . . aerobatics!

I'm s-s-sorry, s-s-sir . . . I'm d-d-doing my b-best . . . It's the f-f-first time I've f-f-flown . . . I'm just the m-m-mechanic!

We'll soon be on their tail, unless . . .

Just as I feared . . . Running into cloud . . .

Rotten visibility . . . We've lost sight of them.

Have to land . . . We're near the coast . . . don't want to drop in the drink.

Doesn't look too rough. I'll have a go . . .

A wall! We're done for!

CRASH
CRACK

?

You all right?

Och, the puir wee laddie! He's fallen into the brambles.

Come ben the hoose. I'll gi'e ye some mair clothes. It's nae far.

A neer thing . . .

That's putting it mildly!

Listen, that's the sound of a plane.

You won't be able to see it in this mist.

We positively insist. Put us down!

But I keep on telling you: I don't know how to land.

The controls, you idiot! Don't take your hands off the wheel!

Whew! I thought my last hour had come.

To be precise: mine too!

In ye go.

Ye'll find a' ye need i' the other room.

Thanks.

?

A'richt?

Fine! I'm coming down.

There!

OH!

41

Snowy! Up to your old tricks again!

That certainly seems to be the best solution . . .

. . . And let this be a lesson, you drunken, disobedient dog!

Our friend has suggested that we spend the night here. It's getting late.

That's an invitation we'll certainly accept. How very kind of you.

Next morning . . .

. . . The dense fog that blanketed the British Isles during the night caused a number of accidents . . .

Off the Scottish coast this morning, fishermen from Kiltoch discovered floating wreckage of a light aircraft registration G-AREI. There was no trace of the crew, who are presumed drowned.

G-AREI! . . . The plane we followed: the same registration . . . Well, that puts paid to that. They're dead, poor devils.

Maybe, but I'd like to be absolutely sure. I'm going to Kiltoch . . . to look around.

It's no above fifteen miles tae Kiltoch. But mind ye keep tae the path thra' the glen.

Thanks!

Fifteen miles: that's quite a step. We shan't get to Kiltoch before evening.

!?

Snowy! Come here!

Wooah!

Wooah! Wooah!

WOOAAH!

WOOAH! ?

WOOAH!

My poor Snowy!

Whatever made you sit on a thistle?

I can smell the sea. We must be fairly close, now.

Look, there's Kiltoch!

'Evening.

I wonder if you could put me up for the night?

Aye, for sure.

That's fine. I'd like something to eat, too, please . . . I've just arrived in Kiltoch . . . and heard about the air crash. Poor fellows. Do you know, have they recovered the bodies?

No, there's no even a sign o' them yet.

And no more there wull be, neether.

? ?

Nivver!

Why not? . . .

Why not, ye say? . . . Ha! Ha! Ha! A'body can see you're no frae these parts, laddie, else ye'd ken for why they'll no be seen agen. Have ye no haird tell o' THE BEAST?

?

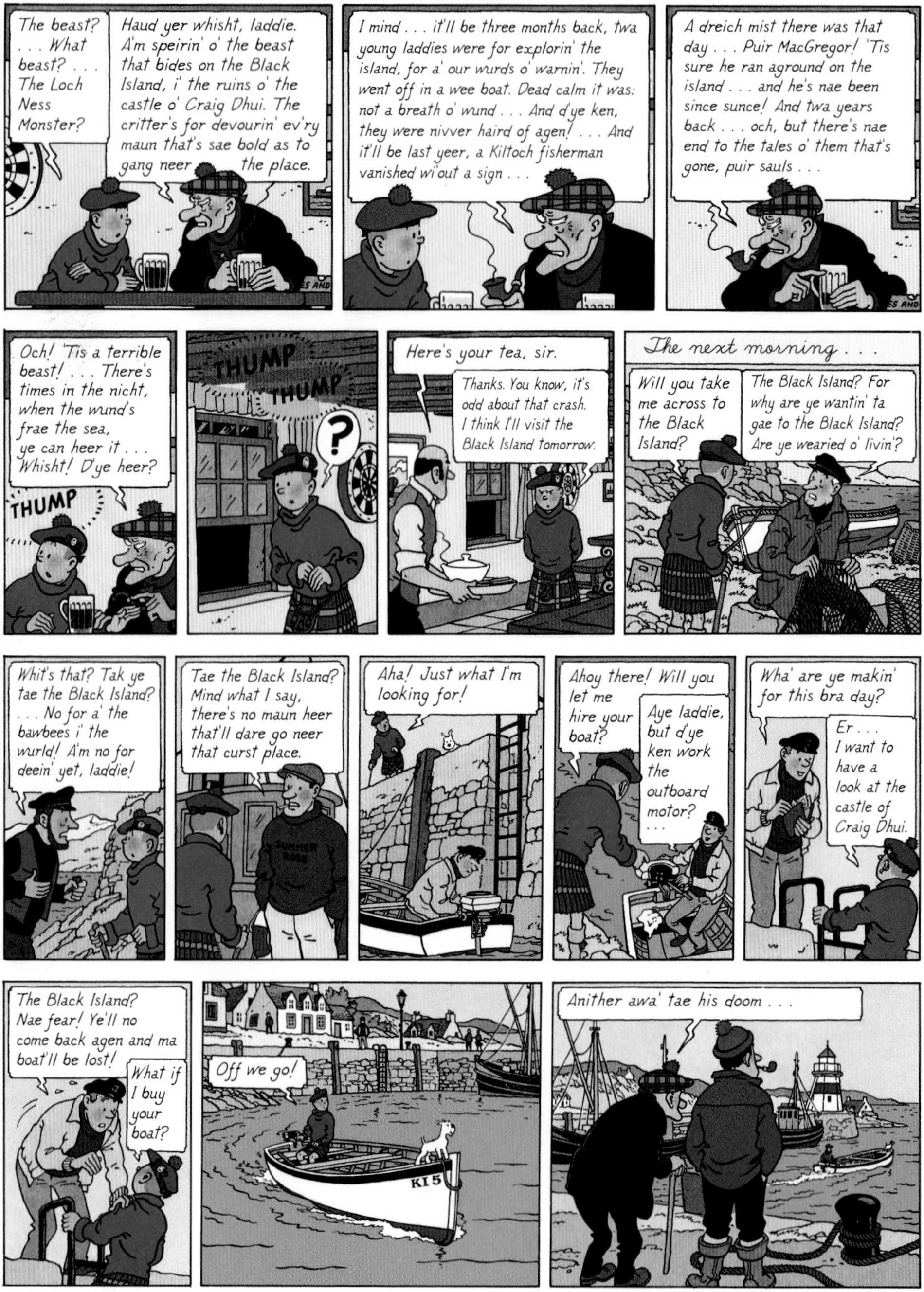

The beast? . . . What beast? . . . The Loch Ness Monster?
Haud yer whisht, laddie. A'm speirin' o' the beast that bides on the Black Island, i' the ruins o' the castle o' Craig Dhui. The critter's for devourin' ev'ry maun that's sae bold as to gang neer the place.
I mind . . . it'll be three months back, twa young laddies were for explorin' the island, for a' our wurds o' warnin'. They went off in a wee boat. Dead calm it was: not a breath o' wund . . . And d'ye ken, they were nivver haird of agen! . . . And it'll be last yeer, a Kiltoch fisherman vanished wi'out a sign . . .
A dreich mist there was that day . . . Puir MacGregor! 'Tis sure he ran aground on the island . . . and he's nae been since sunce! And twa years back . . . och, but there's nae end to the tales o' them that's gone, puir sauls . . .
Och! 'Tis a terrible beast! . . . There's times in the nicht, when the wund's frae the sea, ye can heer it . . . Whisht! D'ye heer?
THUMP
THUMP
THUMP
?
Here's your tea, sir.
Thanks. You know, it's odd about that crash. I think I'll visit the Black Island tomorrow.
The next morning . . .
Will you take me across to the Black Island?
The Black Island? For why are ye wantin' ta gae to the Black Island? Are ye wearied o' livin'?
Whit's that? Tak ye tae the Black Island? . . . No for a' the bawbees i' the wurld! A'm no for deein' yet, laddie!
Tae the Black Island? Mind what I say, there's no maun heer that'll dare go neer that curst place.
SUMMER ROSE
Aha! Just what I'm looking for!
Ahoy there! Will you let me hire your boat?
Aye laddie, but d'ye ken work the outboard motor? . . .
Wha' are ye makin' for this bra day?
Er . . . I want to have a look at the castle of Craig Dhui.
The Black Island? Nae fear! Ye'll no come back agen and ma boat'll be lost!
What if I buy your boat?
Off we go!
KI 5
Anither awa' tae his doom . . .

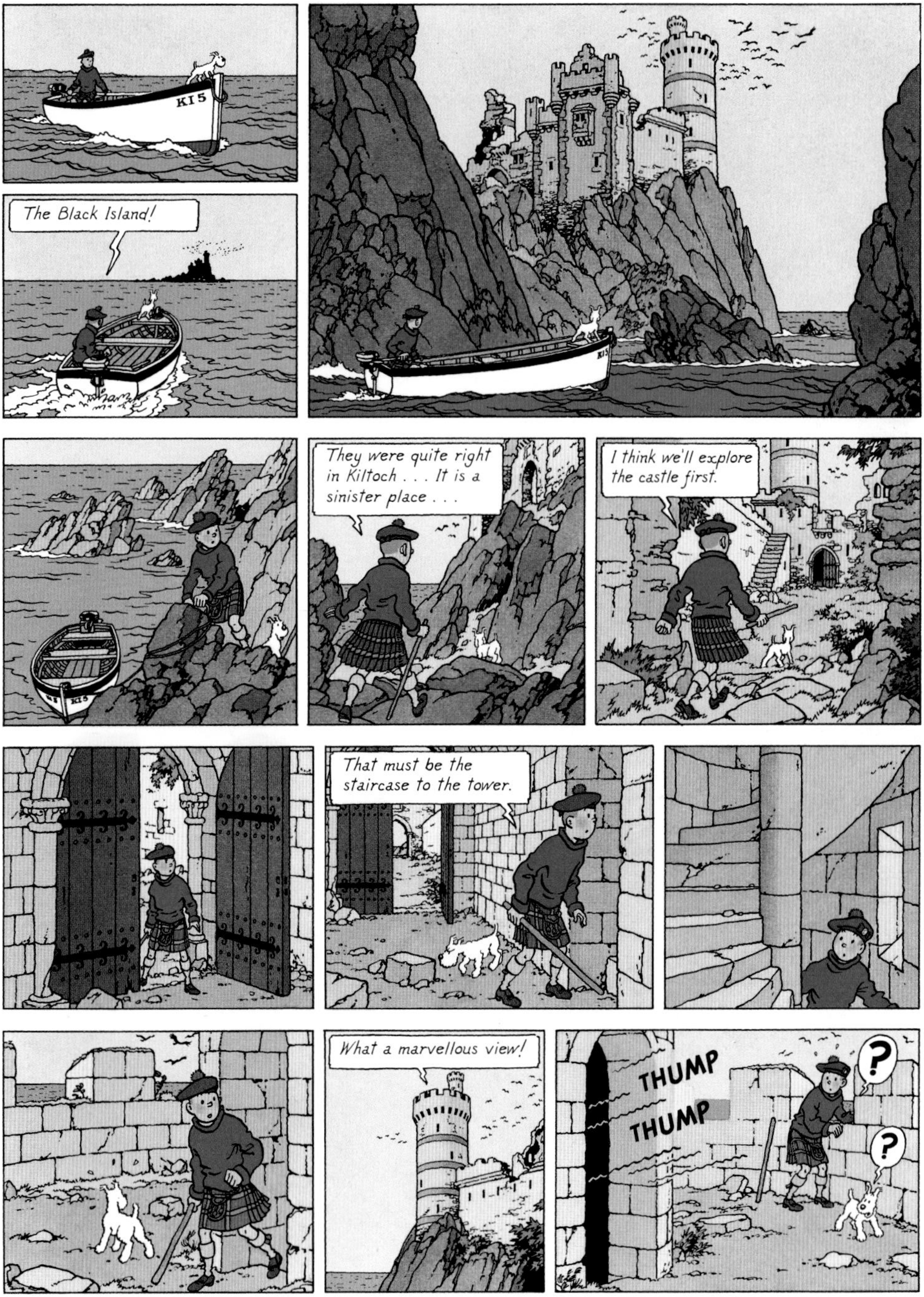
KI 5
The Black Island!
KI 5
KI 5
They were quite right in Kiltoch . . . It is a sinister place . . .
I think we'll explore the castle first.
That must be the staircase to the tower.
What a marvellous view!
THUMP
THUMP
?
?

A gorilla!!

What a monster!

Hit him, Tintin!

Great snakes! The door! It's closed!

It's locked! . . . We're caught in a trap!

Come on, let's find another way out . . .

THUMP

Too late!

If I can't knock him out this time, we're finished!

RHAAH!

Don't miss, Tintin!

Good heavens! He didn't even feel it!

BONK

What's he doing? He seems to be looking for something . . .

Crumbs!

RHAAH! RHAAH!

CRASH

Saved!

Saved!

RHAAH!

WOOAH!

Run for dear life!
Back to the boat!

It's vanished!

What do we do
now, Snowy!

Go on! Seek them,
Ranko! Seek them!

Seek them, Ranko, seek them!

The gorilla! There's a man with him, too.

RHAAH!

WOOAH!

A cave! Well done, Snowy! Perhaps I can squeeze in...

WOOAH!

What a stroke of luck ... it widens out.

Ssh! They're coming ...

Go on, Ranko! ... Go on!

Aha! So that's where he's hiding. We've got him now!

RHAAH!

Help! He's smelt us out! Thank goodness the entrance is so narrow ...

WOOAH

Congratulations, my dear Tintin, you've made a brilliant getaway ...You even managed to evade our faithful Ranko ...You are quite safe in your cave ... Except ...

There's one enemy you won't escape: the sea, my dear Tintin. You have forgotten the sea. The tide is rising. Unless you prefer to come out and meet little Ranko again, you'll drown in your hole like a rat!

We've got to get out of here . . .

BANG
BANG

BANG

He really means business!

WOOAH!

Now what . . . ?

WOOAH!
WOOAH!

What's Snowy found? Let's have a look.

Snowy, you're a marvel! We're saved!

Hello, the cave seems to go on.

Where does this lead . . . ?

A glimmer of light . . .

?

A printing press! The forgers! I never guessed I was so near my goal.

It's a beauty... Absolutely perfect... just look at that thread.

HANDS UP!

? ?

Put your guns on the ground. And don't turn round, or I'll shoot... Come on, you with the boots on. I said put your gun down!

I...I... haven't got one.

Don't try turning round!

Make just one move, either of you, and...

... it'll be the last thing you do!

OH!

THUD

Tintin!

And he wasn't even armed!

Get back! And put up your hands!

That's enough horseplay. There's a coil of rope over there. You, puss-in-boots, bring it here and tie up your friend with the whiskers. And make a good job of it!

Get a move on! Pull that rope tight, as well. I don't want to have to shoot you.

Your turn now... There, that'll do... it's amazing how quickly thugs come to their senses at the wrong end of a loaded gun.

A loaded gun?? ... Of all the stupid clods! ... I've just remembered: there's no ammunition in my pistol!

A fine time to think of that!

Great snakes! He's right. It's completely empty!

Help! Help! ...Rescue!... Help! Help!

Help! ...Help! Tintin's here...Help! Help! ...Help!

Stop that! Shut up, or I'll...

Go ahead... threaten us! Words won't keep us quiet ...Aren't you forgetting that gun isn't loaded?

Maybe. But there's more than one way of using an automatic... I'll demonstrate!

Golly, that's the stuff, Tintin! ... One! ... Two! ...Knockout!

Too late! They've raised the alarm... I can hear footsteps...someone coming...

Quick! An ink roller . . . One of those will be more effective than an empty gun.

? !

No one here!

We're too late, he's gone.

This is Tintin's handiwork, and no mistake! The schweinhund made off when he heard us coming. Go and warn the boss . . . And hurry!

My old friend's . . . Dr Müller . . . and his man Ivan!

?

Ivan! . . . I . . .

THUD

What is it, chief?

Any more? . . . Doesn't look like it . . . Good! That gives me a chance to take care of this lot!

There, that'll do. And be good boys while I'm away!

WOOAAH

Fully loaded: that's better. Still, I hope I shan't need to use it . . . Now, let's go . . .

OK. But mind what you're doing this time!

? ♪♫♪

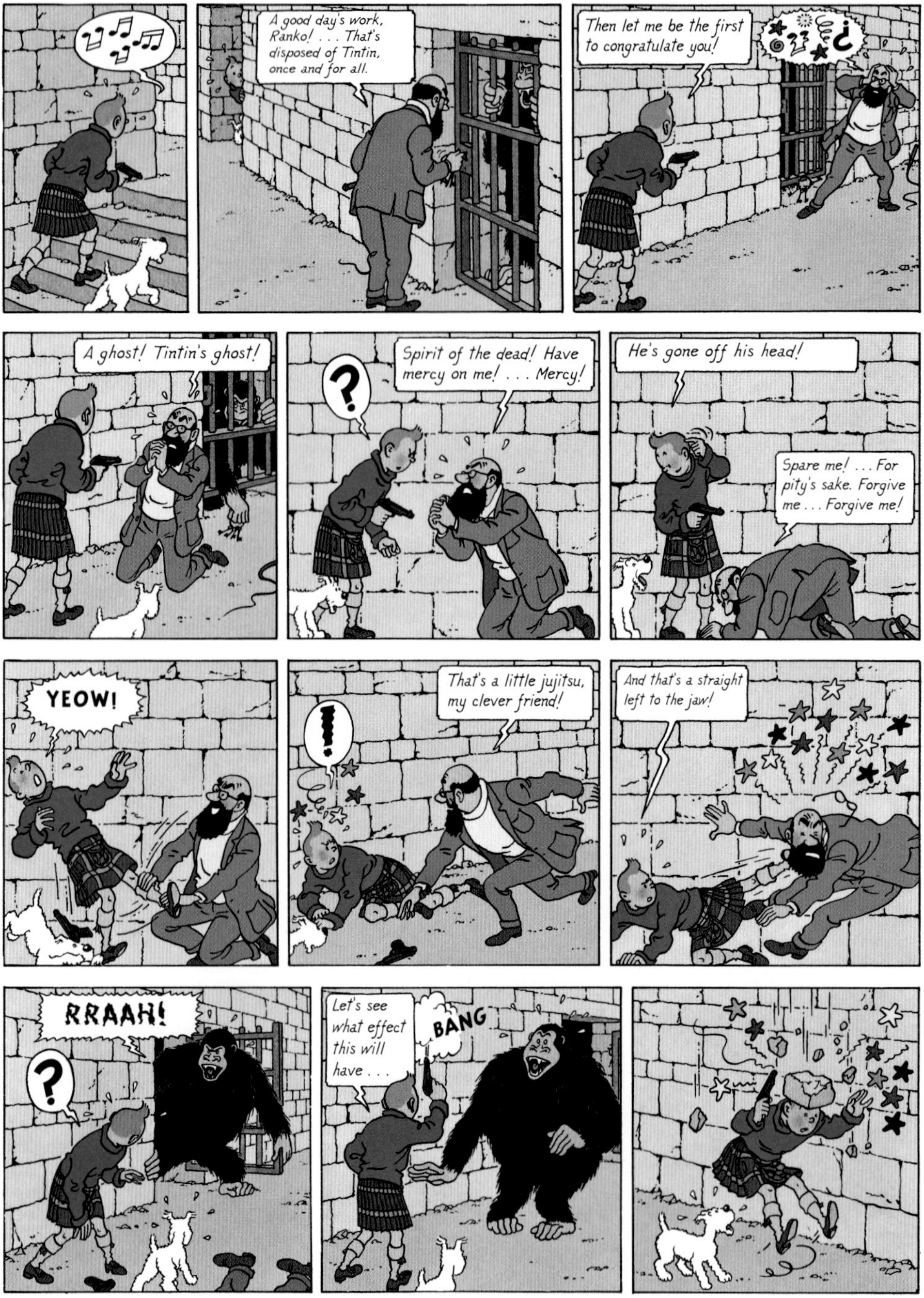
A good day's work, Ranko! . . . That's disposed of Tintin, once and for all.
Then let me be the first to congratulate you!
A ghost! Tintin's ghost!
Spirit of the dead! Have mercy on me! . . . Mercy!
He's gone off his head!
Spare me! . . . For pity's sake. Forgive me . . . Forgive me!
YEOW!
That's a little jujitsu, my clever friend!
And that's a straight left to the jaw!
RRAAH!
Let's see what effect this will have . . .
BANG

OH!

He'll eat Tintin!

WOOAH!

WOOAH!
WOOAH!
WOOAH!

That's got rid of him!
Now to help Tintin.

?

!

Golly, what's the
matter now?

?

!

Oh, it's only him
again...Watch this!

WOOAH!

You frighten him to death, Snowy!

Silly, isn't it? . . .
Imagine, a great big
animal like that scared
out of his wits by a
tiny little . . .

?

Snowy! . . . Snowy! . . . Where are you, Snowy?

Lionheart! . . . Very funny!

Ah, there you are, lionheart! . . . Come on, we've got to search the rest of this place.

Sh! I can hear someone talking . . . on the other side of that door.

He's won the first round, but let's see what happens now . . . He could make a mistake . . . This is it, he's coming towards us . . .

Hand's up!

It's only a television set!

One final loop . . .

. . . and Johnny James, aerobatic champion, comes in to land . . . Just listen to the crowd cheering!

Some sort of air display.

The next item in our telerecording, high speed formation flying by a squadron from R.A.F. Fighter Command.

Let's have a look at that desk . . .

Good heavens! What a stroke of luck: a list of all their contacts! . . . Czechoslovakia, Germany, France, Holland, Austria, . . . All over the place . . . What a catch for the police!

- 3 -

Hans Släszeck
Sdrodjz, 45 - Praha
Otto Steinkopf
Hedemanstrasse, 18 Potsdam
Louis Bonvault
Villa Gai-Soleil
St Germain (S. & O.)
Kees Nieuwenhuis
Zilverdijk, 73 Amsterdam
Werner Schelhammer
. . . Wien

And here comes another competitor . . . Number . . . number . . . Hello, he doesn't seem to be listed on the official programme . . . But what does that matter? . . . He's really terrific! Just look at that! . . . He must have nerves of steel!

This is incredible . . . He's a genius . . . pilots his plane with superb confidence . . . a fantastic series of aerobatics . . .

LAND! In the name of the law!

I . . . I only wish I could!

56

Now the plane comes roaring down, skims over the field and shoots up like a rocket . . .

Stop! We want to get down, d'you hear?

Now he's heading for the ground again . . . and into another flawless loop he goes, then . . . Good heavens! One of the passengers has slipped out of his seat . . . This is terrible!

Whew! What a stunt! That really had us fooled!

And this time he really is coming down . . . He's going to land . . . He's cut the motor . . .

He touches down . . . the plane bounces . . .

. . . and does one last, hair-raising somersault before it comes to rest in the centre of the field.

A clear victory! The judges are unanimous . . . the aerobatic championship is yours!

I mustn't waste time ...Let's see what else they've got ...

A radio transmitter! I'm in luck!

SOS...SOS...Calling the police... Calling the police...This is an emergency...Are you receiving me?...

Police control... Police control... We are receiving you loud and clear... Come in please.

It's that secret transmitter... The one we've been hunting for the past three months...

They can hear me!

Tintin calling the police... Tintin calling...I'm on the Black Island, off Kiltoch. I've rounded up a gang of forgers and am holding them here. Can you send a squad to pick them up?...Over!

Police control...Police control ...Message received and understood. We will send help at once. Good luck, Tintin!... We'll keep in touch with you... Over and out!

Well, that's that! The police will be here soon, then we'll be able to say goodbye to the Black Island.

About time too. I've had enough of this medieval menagerie!

Crumbs! He's managed to free himself!

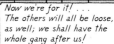

Now we're for it!... The others will all be loose, as well; we shall have the whole gang after us!

Quietly...Quietly...Here, load your guns. I don't want any mistakes this time!

Don't worry, we'll make him pay for what he did to us!

Sssh!

There!

You go round outside and cut off his retreat.

=ZZZING

Got you!

Trapped!

BANG

BANG

He's taken refuge in the tower.

Excellent! We've got him cornered!

Police control... Police control calling Tintin ... We are coming to your assistance... A police launch is heading for the Black Island at full speed. Two detectives are with the officers on board... End of message. Over to you... Tintin... Tintin are you receiving me? ... Come in, please...

Crumbs! No more ammunition!... I'm done for!

Come on! His gun's empty. Bring him down!

Thank goodness I've still got something...

CRACK CRASH

YOW OW

There's the Black Island. Only a few minutes and we'll be ashore.

I'm going to fetch Ranko. At least he won't be put off by a few stones...

That seems to have cooled their enthusiasm...

RRR RRRR

I can hear an engine...

Hooray!... The police!

RRRAH!

!

!

WOOAH

Ranko won't be long!

Ready ... Steady ...

Wait for me!

Go!

If you'd done as I said . . .

Mind the bump! . . .

Drop your guns!

The police! We've had it!

Tintin! You can come out now. It's all right . . . . . . It's us!

Come on, Snowy, our troubles are over ... Down we go!

!

I'm so sorry . . . I tripped over a stone . . .

Oh?

Really?

What happened? Did they put up much of a fight?

No, no . . . To quote Christopher Columbus . . . er . . . Captain Cook . . . er . . . well, someone about that time: "We came, we saw, we conquered!"

Splendid! . . . Before we go, I want to have a last look round. Why don't you come with me?

A plane!

But what about an airfield? How did they . . . er . . . land?

We shall see. There's a door over there, with a steel shutter.

The beach at low tide . . . You see? That was their airstrip.

Here's another lot of those sacks, full of forged notes ready for dispatch.

Brrr! It's cold down here. Let's go on up.

Between ourselves, I shan't be sorry to leave this place . . . I . . . er . . . Do you . . . er . . . believe in ghosts?

Me? . . . Believe in ghosts? Ha! Ha! H . . .

WOO HOO HOOO OO

A g-g-ghost! To be p-p-precise: a s-s-sp-spook!

A ghost? ... The castle haunted? ... What are they babbling about? ...

WOO-HOO

TINTIN!

T-TINTIN!

It's all right. You can come up now. There's no danger: and no ghost!

It was this poor old chap howling. He broke his arm falling down the tower staircase, just before you arrived. We're the best of friends, now.

W-what are you going to do with him?

Take him with us if we leave him here the poor beast will starve to death. Far better find him a comfortable home in a zoo.

Come on, let's go. The launch is waiting for us.

Meanwhile...

Aye, sirs, ye can pu' it in your newspapers that they blackguards'd nivver've been ta'en but fer me. A' says tae yon wee laddie, a' says, "Awa' wi' ye. There's somethin' gey queer afoot on yon Black Island," a' says. "And whit aboot yon beast?" says he. "A muckle o' lies," a' says. "Ye'll nae be findin' a beast, nae mair than in this bar." That's whit a' tells him and he's up and awa'.

They're coming!

Hooray!

Come on!

Good old Tintin!

Welcome back, sir. Can we have a few details? Your own words ...

I ... er ... Well, I ...

How very odd! Did I say something wrong?

The Daily Reporter

GLASGOW EDITION

NO. 11,432

PRICE 4d.

Young Reporter Hero of Black Island Drama

FORGERS FOUND ON MYSTERY ISLE

Full story page five

Police Swoop on International Gang EXCLUSIVE PICTURES

FORGED notes so perfect even bank cashiers are fooled.

At Kiltoch, handcuffed gang leaders are escorted to waiting Black Maria.

A sea dash by police ended in five arrests. Seen with hero reporter Tintin and lion-hearted dog Snowy, from left, Constables E. McGregor, T. W. Stewart, B. Robertson, A. MacLeod.

Black Island 'Beast' Ranko says goodbye to rescuer Tintin in a Glasgow zoo. Once trained to kill intruders at gang hideout, the monster gorilla, injured in battle on

Next morning...

You aren't coming back with me by air?

By air?...No thank you...To be precise: we don't find the pilots entirely...reliable!

Au revoir!

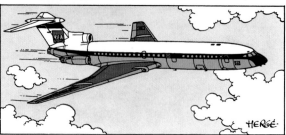

HERGÉ.

HERGÉ
★
THE ADVENTURES OF
TINTIN
★

KING OTTOKAR'S SCEPTRE

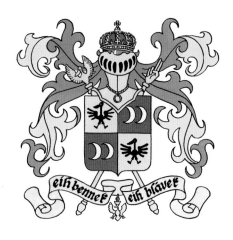

eih bennek ★ eih blávek

EGMONT

KING OTTOKAR'S SCEPTRE

Let's sit down on this bench for a minute.

Hello, someone has left his brief-case behind.

I can't see anybody . . .

Perhaps I ought to open it? The owner's name might be inside.

Here it is! . . . 'Hector Alembick, 24, Flyaway Road'.

That's not far. I'll take it back.

You're making a mistake, Tintin! . . . No good ever comes of getting mixed up in other people's business.

Professor Alembick? Third floor, first door on the right . . .

RAT TAT TAT

Come in!

Oh, good-evening, Mrs Piggott. Put it all on the little table, will you?

It's not Mrs Piggott, Professor. I've brought back your brief-case.

What? . . .

My brief-case?

Ssh! Someone's just come to see him . . .

How very kind of you to return it. I'm especially grateful, as the text of the paper I am reading to the I.S.A. Congress tonight is in there.

The I.S.A.?

I.S.A.: International Sigillographical Association.

Sigi . . . what?

Sigillography. Do you mean you've never heard of it? It's the science concerned with the study of seals. It's extremely interesting and . . . A cigarette?

No thank you: I don't smoke.

Yes, sigillography is an absorbing study. One look at my collection will convince you.

?

WOOAH

Oh, good gracious! I'm so sorry! I have a dreadful habit of dropping my cigarette ends about!

This is one of the rarest items in my collection: the seal of Charlemagne. Here is the seal of Edward the Confessor, and next to it one which belonged to Gradenigo, Doge of Venice. And here's another fine specimen: an intaglio ring from the Saxon period.

. . . And this is a very unusual seal, which I found quite by chance in Prague. It is the seal of Ottokar IV, King of Syldavia . . .

Oh? . . .

68

It is one of the few seals we know of from that country. But there must be others, and I am going to Syldavia to study the problem on the spot.

The Syldavian Ambassador, an old friend of mine, has promised to give me letters of introduction. I hope I shall be allowed to go through the historic national archives. A cigarette? . . .

No, thank you . . . And when are you leaving?

As soon as I have found a secretary. At least, rather more than a secretary; I really need someone to take care of all the details of my journey, like hotels, passports, luggage and so on.

But I see that you have become interested in sigillography too. Let me have your name and address and I will send you my booklet: 'How to become a sigillographer.'

How very kind of you . . .

He's going . . . Quick, meet him on the stairs . . .

Steady! . . . Here he comes!

That's a funny place to put a watch right . . .

Got it! . . . Wonderful, the way a miniature camera can be hidden in a watch . . .

Here! . . . .

We'll develop the picture right away.

Is it OK?

⁉

69

Bother! I've left my book at Professor Alembick's flat.

Anyway, we know his name is Tintin.

2nd FLOOR

?

Tintin! . . . Tintin! . . . You know that a name by itself won't do . . . We must have a photograph!

Well, I've had enough . . . I'm off . . . If anyone wants me, I'm at the 'KLOW'! . . . Goodbye! . . .

Goodbye!

24

This is all very mysterious . . . Let's follow him.

- KLOW -
S VIAN RESTAURANT

LOW -

RESTAURAN

Well, well! 'Syldavian Restaurant'. The plot thickens!

Let's go in!

·KLOW·

Hello? . . . Where's he gone?

A customer! . . .

Er . . . I'd like . . . something to eat . . . please . . .

Will you take a seat, sir? . . .

What would you like, sir? . . .

Er . . . bring me . . . er . . . a 'szlaszeck' with mushrooms . . . and a glass of 'szpradj' . . .

But I'd like a wash first . . .

The cloakroom is at the end of the passage.

GENTLEMEN

. . . As for Professor Alembick, we'll have to wait for a day or two, until he's got the papers from the Embassy . . .

!

Ahem!

!

At the end of the passage, sir . . .

I'm sorry, I misunderstood.

Did he catch me listening at the door?

. . . and he was listening outside the door! He's a young chap with a funny tuft of hair . . . There's a dog with him . . .

I'll bet a thousand khors it's the fellow Sporovitch tried to photograph! . . .

Where's Snowy got to? . . .

TING
TING
TING

My bill, please . . .

In a moment, sir . . .

·KLOW·
SYLDAVIAN RESTAURANT
38, NIGHTINGALE ROAD
PROP: J. KNOSZVITCH

1 Szlaszeck davy · 1·20
                    ·60
1 Szpäs   1·80
                    ·18
Servia 10%   1·98

Danger awaits the one who dares
To poke his nose in others' affairs
~ SYLDAVIAN PROVERB ~

What does this mean?

What, sir? . . . Oh, yes . . . Don't you know
the old Syldavian custom, sir? . . .
In restaurants in my country
there's always a proverb or a
short motto on the bill.

Oh, really?

Yes, sir. Rather nice, isn't it? . . .
Thank you, just right . . . I hope
you enjoyed your meal, sir? . . .

Very much, thank you.
Your 'szlaszeck' was
excellent. How do
you make it?

Ah, it's one of our specialities: the
hind leg of a young dog in
Syldavian sauce . . .

SNOWY!

SNOWY!
SNOWY!

Ah, there you are! . . .
Where have you been
hiding?

I hope you will come again, sir.

Ha! ha! ha! We shan't see
him again in a hurry!

SERVICE

(72)

Well I'm
. . . !

Odd! All very
odd! . . .

HIC

HIC

A few minutes later . . .

Suf . . . Sur . . . Syb . . . Ah,
here it is! Syldavia: a State
in the Balkan Peninsula. In
the XIIth century Syldavia
was conquered by the
Bordurians.

RRRRING
RRRRING
RRRRING

Hello? . . . Yes, it's me . . . Yes of course
it's me . . . I . . . Who are you? . . .
What? You'll tell me later? . . . Can you
come and see me? What about? . . . Oh!
. . . All right, I'll   expect you about
half past eight   . . . Goodbye . . .

A man with a foreign
accent, with something
very   important
to tell   me . . . ?

HIC

In 1275 the people of Syldavia rose
against the Bordurians, and in 1277 the
revolutionary leader, Baron Almaszout,
was proclaimed King. He adopted the title
of Ottokar the First, but should not be
confused with Premysl Ottakar the First,
the duke who became King of Bohemia in
the XIIth century.

HIC

Twenty past eight.
My mysterious foreigner
should soon be here.

TINTIN

RRRING

HIC

?

(73)

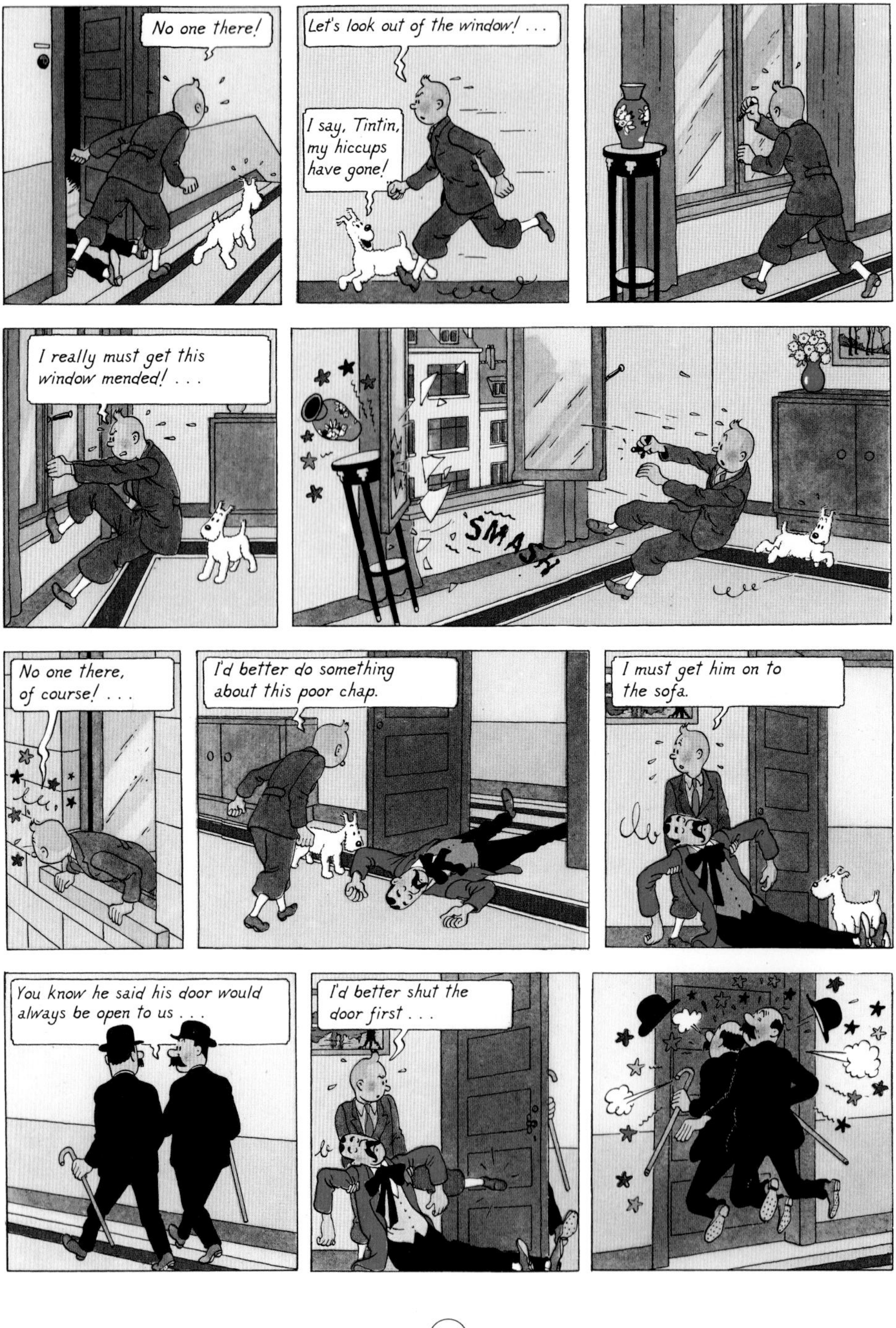
No one there!
Let's look out of the window! . . .
I say, Tintin, my hiccups have gone!
I really must get this window mended! . . .
SMASH
No one there, of course! . . .
I'd better do something about this poor chap.
I must get him on to the sofa.
You know he said his door would always be open to us . . .
I'd better shut the door first . . .

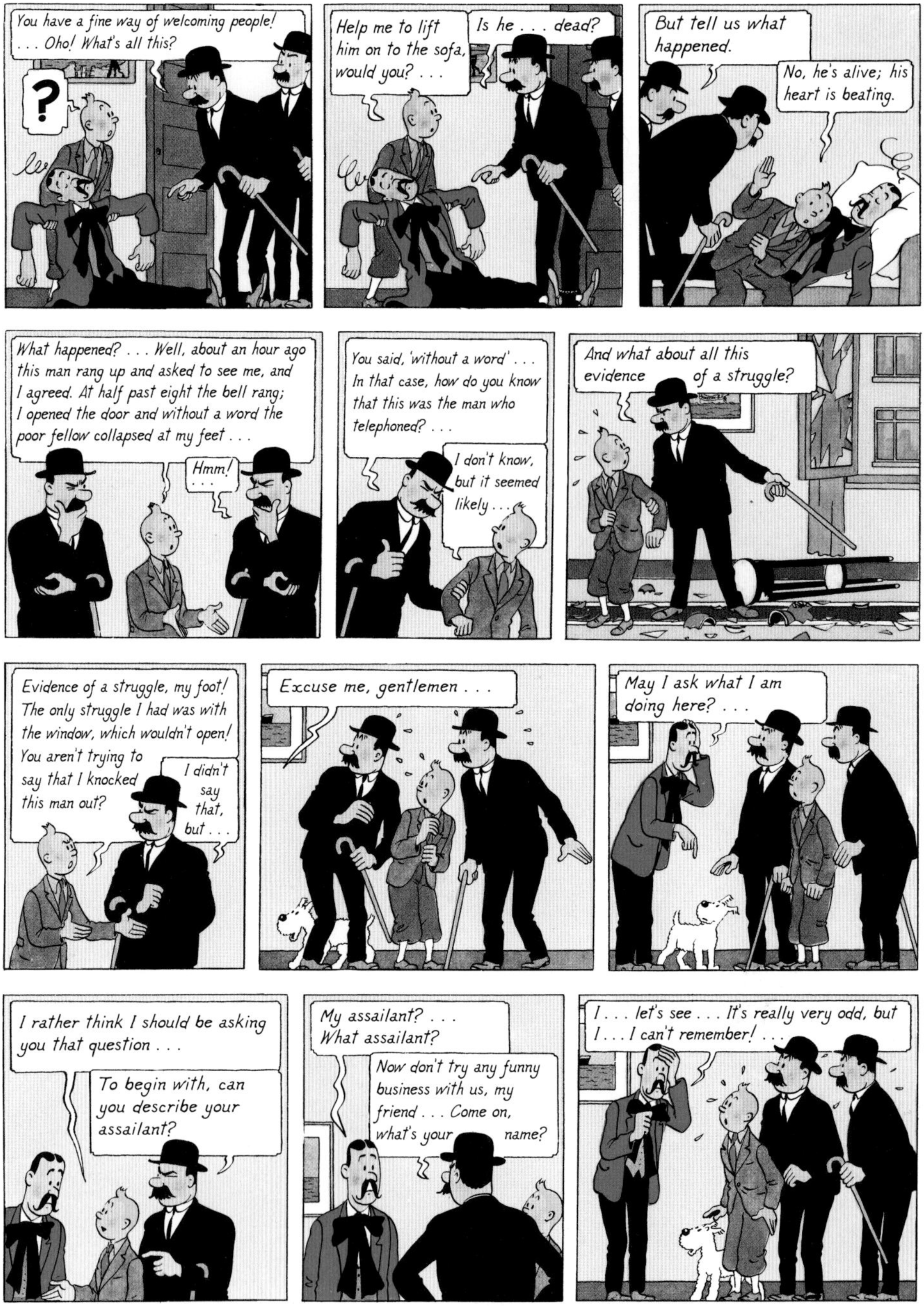
You have a fine way of welcoming people! . . . Oho! What's all this?
?
Help me to lift him on to the sofa, would you? . . .
Is he . . . dead?
But tell us what happened.
No, he's alive; his heart is beating.
What happened? . . . Well, about an hour ago this man rang up and asked to see me, and I agreed. At half past eight the bell rang; I opened the door and without a word the poor fellow collapsed at my feet . . .
Hmm! . . .
You said, 'without a word' . . . In that case, how do you know that this was the man who telephoned? . . .
I don't know, but it seemed likely . . .
And what about all this evidence of a struggle?
Evidence of a struggle, my foot! The only struggle I had was with the window, which wouldn't open! You aren't trying to say that I knocked this man out?
I didn't say that, but . . .
Excuse me, gentlemen . . .
May I ask what I am doing here? . . .
I rather think I should be asking you that question . . .
To begin with, can you describe your assailant?
My assailant? . . . What assailant?
Now don't try any funny business with us, my friend . . . Come on, what's your name?
I . . . let's see . . . It's really very odd, but I . . . I can't remember! . . .

For the last time, my man, don't try any funny business with us... What's your name?

Out with it!... And get a move on!

What if he's telling the truth and he really is suffering from amnesia?

What has anaemia to do with it?...

Amnesia!... He probably had a violent shock that made him lose his memory! It's always happening. If I were you I'd take him to a hospital and let a doctor have a look at him...

Hmm!... What do you think?...

Hmm!... We could try...

You know, I can't really believe in this magnesia...

It's all very odd... I just can't make head or tail of this business...

Anyway, I'd better get a new window pane put in...

Hello, is that the builder? ... Could you replace a pane of glass for me? Yes ... Tintin... You'll come tonight?... Splendid!...

RRRRRING

Oh, it's you! Come in.

There...

Thanks

Goodnight Mr Tintin. Always glad to help!...

Glad to help!... Not again for a long time, I hope...

!?! ?*!

SMASH

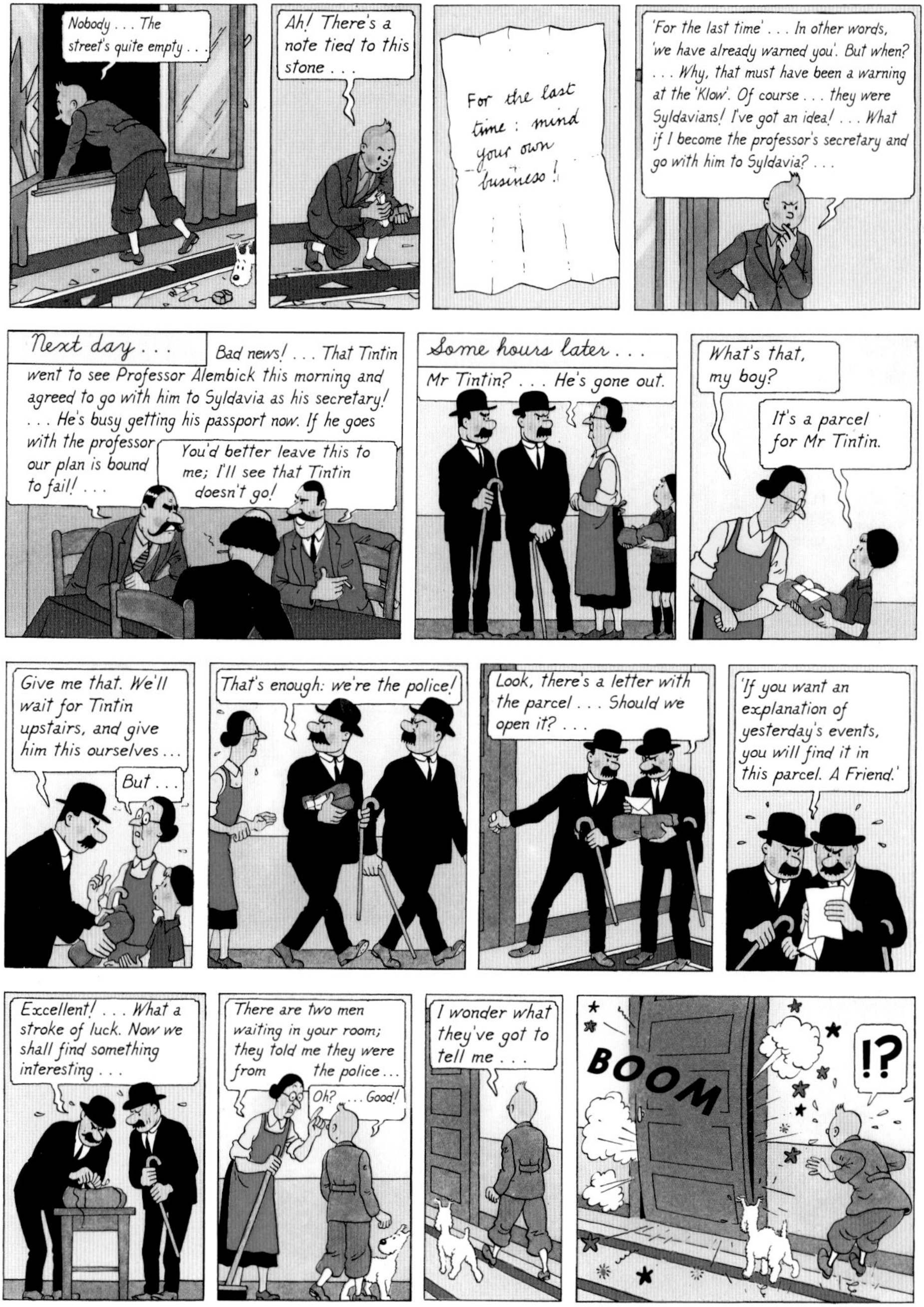
Nobody . . . The street's quite empty . . .
Ah! There's a note tied to this stone . . .
For the last time: mind your own business!
'For the last time' . . . In other words, 'we have already warned you'. But when? . . . Why, that must have been a warning at the 'Klow'. Of course . . . they were Syldavians! I've got an idea! . . . What if I become the professor's secretary and go with him to Syldavia? . . .
Next day . . .
Bad news! . . . That Tintin went to see Professor Alembick this morning and agreed to go with him to Syldavia as his secretary! . . . He's busy getting his passport now. If he goes with the professor our plan is bound to fail! . . .
You'd better leave this to me; I'll see that Tintin doesn't go!
Some hours later . . .
Mr Tintin? . . . He's gone out.
What's that, my boy?
It's a parcel for Mr Tintin.
Give me that. We'll wait for Tintin upstairs, and give him this ourselves . . .
But . . .
That's enough: we're the police!
Look, there's a letter with the parcel . . . Should we open it? . . .
'If you want an explanation of yesterday's events, you will find it in this parcel. A Friend.'
Excellent! . . . What a stroke of luck. Now we shall find something interesting . . .
There are two men waiting in your room; they told me they were from the police . . .
Oh? . . . Good!
I wonder what they've got to tell me . . .
BOOM
!?

There it goes! BOOM

?

What have you done? What's happened? . . .

Er . . . there was a parcel for you . . .

. . . and a letter . . . Here: read it . . . We opened the parcel. We heard a 'fizz' and we just had time to throw it away, or it would have blown up in our faces!

Let's get nearer; we can mix with the crowd . . .

A bomb! . . . The cunning scoundrels! . . . They wanted to kill me!

!?

Quick, downstairs! . . . The men who did it are out there! . . .

Hurry! Hurry!

There they are!

It's him!

Quick . . . Start her up! . . . I'll hold them off!

Look out! . . .

BANG

Give me a gun . . .

BANG

Too late! . . . They've got away!

There's a motor bike! . . . We've got to follow them!

Get going! We're all set! . . .

To be precise: we're all set!

Right! . . .

Whatever happens, hang on tight!

He's alone! ... We'll fix him! ...
Let him gradually close up on us ...

We're catching up!

Now we've got 'em! ...

Now then, jam on the brakes ... Wham! ...

!?

This time I think we've really shaken him off for good.

Where's Snowy? . . . And the others? . . . What's happened to them?

It can't be true! Surely . . . yes, it's them! . . . Where have they come from?

You started off so suddenly that we . . . we couldn't keep up with you. So we commandeered this car. Shall we follow them? . . .

It's no good: they're too far ahead.

I'll leave you here. I must go and pack my things at once. I am going to Syldavia tomorrow.

RRRRING
RRRRING
RRRRING
RRRRING

RRRRING

Hello? . . . Yes . . . Ah, good-evening, Professor . . . Yes, everything is ready for our trip . . . Yes, I have booked seats on the Klow plane . . . We'll meet at the airport in the morning, at 11 o'clock . . .

We go via Prague, yes . . . Well, goodbye till tomorrow, Professor . . . Yes . . . I . . . Hello? . . . Hello? . . . Hello? . . .

Oooooh . . . Help! . . . Help! . . . Aaaaaah! . . .

?

The professor is in danger! Quick! quick! There's not a moment to lose! . . .

I only hope I'm not too late! . . .

?¿★★! !★✱~! !★!

Ah! It's you, Tintin. Have you come to help me finish my packing? . . .

I . . . I'm sorry, but I don't understand! . . . I thought I heard you cry out and shout for help . . . So I rushed straight round . . .

Me shouting for help? . . . I'm afraid I don't know what you're talking about.

But it's extraordinary! . . . I can't have been dreaming! . . . I quite definitely heard shouts for help . . .

Next morning . . .

It's very kind of you to come and see me off.

But of course we've come . . .

To be precise: of course . . .

Professor, may I introduce Mr Thomson and Mr Thompson, of the C.I.D. . . . Professor Alembick, sigillographer.

How do you do?

Very well, thank you.

Oh, you've got new hats?

Yes, aren't they smart? . . . Pure English felt, extra-light: only £3·95. Wonderful bargain!

All passengers for Prague, this way please . . .

Well, goodbye, and bon voyage! . . .

And good luck in Syldavia!

Thanks.

Compression! Petrol on! Contact!

Come and look what a pretty picture these sheep make . . . down in that field.

Can you see them, down there?

Yes . . . How tiny they are: you can hardly see them . . .

?

How odd . . .

Are we landing? . . .

Yes: it's Frankfurt. They touch down for a few minutes.

Mr Alembick? There's a telegram for you.

Aha! . . .

Here's some good news . . . The Syldavian government has put a special aircraft at our disposal. Look . . .

'Professor Alembick, passenger aboard aircraft No.573 OO-AGE. Frankfurt Airport. Special plane for Klow will meet you at Prague. Stop. Best wishes' . . . It's signed Schzlozitch, Air Minister . . .

Sweets . . . Sandwiches . . . Chocolates . . . Cigarettes . . .

I think they're calling us . . .

?

All passengers for Prague, please take your seats in the aircraft . . .

OO-AGE

It's really very odd . . .

Oh, well, let's forget it and look at this brochure . . .

SYLDAVIA
KINGDOM OF THE BLACK PELICAN

SYLDAVIA
THE KINGDOM OF THE BLACK PELICAN

AMONG the many enchanting places which deservedly attract foreign visitors with a love for picturesque ceremony and colourful folklore, there is one small country which, although relatively unknown, surpasses many others in interest. Isolated until modern times because of its inaccessible position, this country is now served by a regular air-line network, which brings it within the reach of all who love unspoiled beauty, the proverbial hospitality of a peasant people, and the charm of medieval customs which still survive despite the march of progress.

This is Syldavia.

Syldavia is a small country in Eastern Europe, comprising two great valleys: those of the river Vladir, and its tributary, the Moltus. The rivers meet at Klow, the capital (122,000 inhabitants). These valleys are flanked by wide plateaux covered with forests, and are surrounded by high, snow-capped mountains. In the fertile Syldavian plains are cornlands and cattle pastures. The subsoil is rich in minerals of all kinds.

Numerous thermal and sulphur springs gush from the earth, the chief centres being at Klow (cardiac diseases) and Kragoniedin (rheumatic complaints).

The total population is estimated to be 642,000 inhabitants.

Syldavia exports wheat, mineral-water from Klow, firewood, horses and violinists.

HISTORY OF SYLDAVIA

Until the VIth century, Syldavia was inhabited by nomadic tribes of unknown origin.

Overrun by the Slavs in the VIth century, the country was conquered in the Xth century by the Turks, who drove the Slavs into the mountains and occupied the plains.

In 1127, Hveghi, leader of a Slav tribe, swooped down from the mountains at the head of a band of partisans and fell upon isolated Turkish villages, putting all who resisted him to the sword. Thus he rapidly became master of a large part of Syldavian territory.

A great battle took place in the valley of the Moltus near Zileheroum, the Turkish capital of Syldavia, between the Turkish army and Hveghi's irregulars.

Enfeebled by long inactivity and badly led by incompetent officers, the Turkish army put up little resistance and fled in disorder.

Having vanquished the Turks, Hveghi was elected king, and given the name Muskar, that is, The Brave (Muskh: 'brave' and Kar: 'king').

The capital, Zileheroum, was renamed Klow, that is, Freetown, (Kloho: 'to free', and Ow: 'town').

A typical fisherman from Dbrnouk (south coast of Syldavia)

Guard at the Royal Treasure House, Klow

Syldavian peasant on her way to market

◀

A view of Niedzdrow, in the Vladir valley ▶

THE BATTLE OF ZILEHEROUM
After a XVth century miniature

H.M. King Muskar XII, the present ruler of Syldavia in the uniform of Colonel of the Guards

him a blow on the head with the sceptre, laying him low and at the same time crying in Syldavian: '*Eih bennek, eih blavek!*', which can be said to mean: 'If you gather thistles, expect prickles'. And turning to his astonished court he said: '*Honi soit qui mal y pense!*'

Then, gazing intently at his sceptre, he addressed it in the following words: 'O Sceptre, thou has saved my life. Be henceforward the true symbol of Syldavian Kingship. Woe to the king who loses thee, for I declare that such a man shall be unworthy to rule thereafter.'

And from that time, every year on St. Vladimir's Day each successor of Ottokar IV has made a great ceremonial tour of his capital.

He bears in his hand the historic sceptre, without which he would lose the right to rule; as he passes, the people sing the famous anthem:

Syldavians unite!
Praise our King's might:
The Sceptre his right!

Right: The sceptre of Ottokar IV

Below: An illuminated page from 'The Memorable Deeds of Ottokar IV', a XIVth century manuscript

Muskar was a wise king who lived at peace with his neighbours, and the country prospered. He died in 1168, mourned by all his subjects.

His eldest son succeeded to the throne with the title of Muskar II.

Unlike his father, Muskar II lacked authority and was unable to keep order in his kingdom. A period of anarchy replaced one of peaceful prosperity.

In the neighbouring state of Borduria the people observed Syldavia's decline, and their king profited by this opportunity to invade the country. Borduria annexed Syldavia in 1195.

For almost a century Syldavia groaned under the foreign yoke. In 1275 Baron Almaszout repeated the exploits of Hveghi by coming down from the hills and routing the Bordurians in less than six months.

He was proclaimed King in 1277, taking the name of Ottokar. He was, however, much less powerful than Muskar.

The barons who had helped him in the campaign against the Bordurians forced him to grant them a charter, based on the English Magna Carta signed by King John (Lackland). This marked the beginning of the feudal system in Syldavia.

Ottokar I of Syldavia should not be confused with the Ottakars (Premysls) who were Dukes, and later Kings, of Bohemia.

This period was noteworthy for the rise in power of the nobles, who fortified their castles and maintained bands of armed mercenaries, strong enough to oppose the King's forces.

But the true founder of the kingdom of Syldavia was Ottokar IV, who ascended the throne in 1370.

From the time of his accession he initiated widespread reforms. He raised a powerful army and subdued the arrogant nobles, confiscating their wealth.

He fostered the advancement of the arts, of letters, commerce and agriculture.

He united the whole nation and gave it that security, both at home and abroad, so necessary for the renewal of prosperity.

It was he who pronounced those famous words: '*Eih bennek, eih blavek*', which have become the motto of Syldavia.

The origin of this saying is as follows:

One day Baron Staszrvich, son of one of the dispossessed nobles whose lands had been forfeited to the crown, came before the sovereign and recklessly claimed the throne of Syldavia.

The King listened in silence, but when the presumptuous baron's speech ended with a demand that he deliver up his sceptre, the King rose and cried fiercely: 'Come and get it!'

Mad with rage, the young baron drew his sword, and before the retainers could intervene, fell upon the King.

The King stepped swiftly aside, and as his adversary passed him, carried forward by the impetus of his charge, Ottokar struck

Well, that's all very interesting, but . . .

. . . I must be on my guard. Without his glasses this man can pick out a flock of sheep from as high up as this. He has good eyes for a short-sighted person! . . . And another strange thing: ever since I found him packing his bags I haven't seen him smoke a single cigarette.

. . . Unless I'm very much mistaken, I'm travelling with an impostor! . . . If that's so, then everything fits in . . . The shouts I heard on the telephone were from the real Professor Alembick. He has been kidnapped and this man has taken his place.

He must be exposed! At Prague I'll pull off that false beard, and have him arrested!

Prague? . . . Already?

Yes, we are landing . . .

Now's my chance!

OH!

OUCH!

?

I . . . I'm sorry . . . I . . . I missed a step . . . I beg your pardon . . .

D-don't mention it! . . .

Professor Alembick? . . . Your special plane is waiting.

It's a real beard!

But what about his glasses? . . . Not that that proves anything. Plenty of people can see better at a distance than near to . . . As for the cigarettes, perhaps he has simply given up smoking . . .

You see, Snowy, in rough weather when the plane bumps about you fasten yourself into the seat like this . . .

There is the frontier . . . We are now over Syldavia . . .

What lovely country . . .

Very pretty, isn't it? I'll let you admire it a bit more closely . . .

There! . . . Happy landings! . . .

TINTIN?!

Quick, the parachute! . . .

No time to buckle it on! . . .

Mind the jerk when it opens! . . .

Zrälükʒ! . . .

Wooah!

Czesʒtot on klebcʒ!

Splendid! . . . Snowy fell into the parachute . . . He's safe!

My aeroplane . . . BRRRR . . . I fell . . . Crash! . . . Into the straw . . .

Czestot wzruzkar nietz on vaghabontz! . . . Czestot bätczer yhzer kzömmetz noh dascz politzski?

Snowy! Snowy!

Wooah! Wooah!

Kzommet micz omhz, noh dascz politzski!

Come with you to the police? . . . With pleasurski! . . . I've got a complaint to make!

ГЕНДАРМАСКАИА

Captain, what I have to say is of the utmost importance . . . May I speak to you in private? . . .

Er . . . Yes . . . Leave us alone . . .

First, may I ask you a question? . . . I read in a brochure about Syldavia that if your King loses his sceptre he will be forced to abdicate. Is that true? . . .

As a matter of fact it is . . . But how does this concern you?

I'll tell you. I am certain there's a conspiracy against King Muskar XII, and that certain people will try to steal the sceptre from him!

What's that you say? . . . What makes you imagine such a thing?

I'll explain . . . But first, are you sure we are not overheard?

Definitely not. Go on . . .

This must be serious. They've been in there nearly an hour . . .

You have just rendered a great service to my country: I thank you. I will telegraph at once to Klow and have Professor Alembick arrested. I'm sure I can rely on you for absolute secrecy . . .

Of course . . . But I must be on my way . . . Can I hire a car?

There isn't a single car in the village. But tomorrow is market-day in Klow. You can go with a peasant who is leaving here today. But you won't arrive there until morning . . .

Too bad, but I have no choice. I'll go with the peasant.

Hello? . . . Yes, this is Klow 3324 . . . Yes, Central Committee . . . Trovik speaking . . . Oh it's you Wizskitotz . . . What? . . . Tintin? . . . But that's impossible: the pilot has just told me . . . What? . . . Into some straw! . . . Szplug! He must be prevented from reaching Klow at all costs! . . . Do it how you like . . . Yes, ring up Sirov . . .

Hello? . . . Yes, this is Sirov . . . Hello Wizskitotz . . . Yes . . . A young boy, on the road to Klow . . . In a peasant's cart . . . Good, we'll be waiting in the forest . . . Yes, we'll leave at once . . . Goodbye! . . .

Look out! . . . Here they come! . . .

Hands up! . . .

?

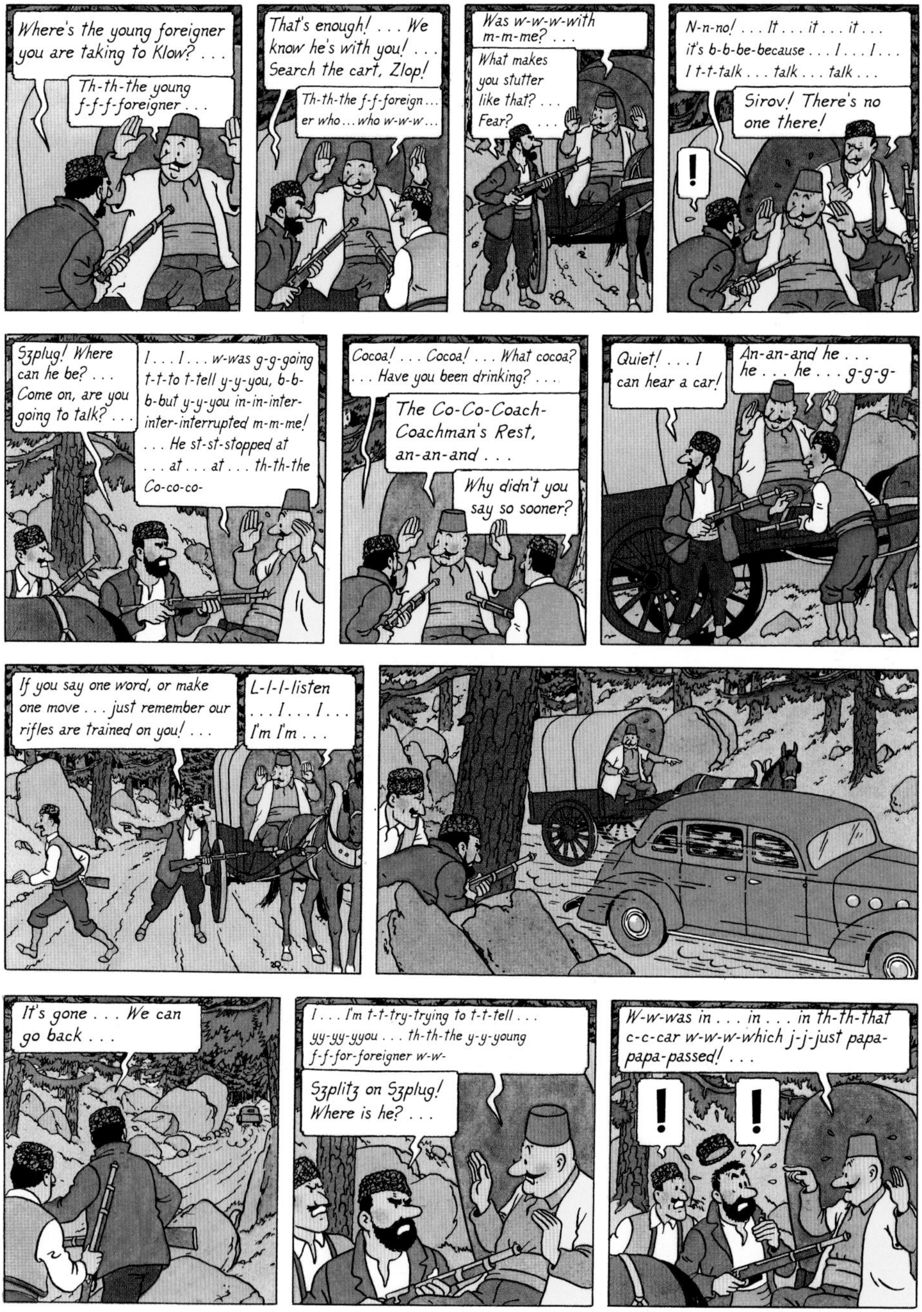
Where's the young foreigner you are taking to Klow? . . .
Th-th-the young f-f-f-foreigner . . .
That's enough! . . . We know he's with you! . . . Search the cart, Zlop!
Th-th-the f-f-foreign . . . er who . . . who w-w-w . . .
Was w-w-w-with m-m-me? . . .
What makes you stutter like that? . . . Fear?
N-n-no! . . . It . . . it . . . it . . . it's b-b-be-because . . . I . . . I . . . I t-t-talk . . . talk . . . talk . . .
Sirov! There's no one there!
!
Szplug! Where can he be? . . . Come on, are you going to talk? . . .
I . . . I . . . w-was g-g-going t-t-to t-tell y-y-you, b-b-b-but y-y-you in-in-inter-inter-interrupted m-m-me! . . . He st-st-stopped at . . . at . . . at . . . th-th-the Co-co-co-
Cocoa! . . . Cocoa! . . . What cocoa? . . . Have you been drinking? . . .
The Co-Co-Coach-Coachman's Rest, an-an-and . . .
Why didn't you say so sooner?
Quiet! . . . I can hear a car!
An-an-and he . . . he . . . he . . . g-g-g-
If you say one word, or make one move . . . just remember our rifles are trained on you! . . .
L-l-l-listen . . . I . . . I . . . I'm I'm . . .
It's gone . . . We can go back . . .
I . . . I'm t-t-try-trying to t-t-tell . . . yy-yy-yyou . . . th-th-the y-y-young f-f-for-foreigner w-w-
Szplitz on Szplug! Where is he? . . .
W-w-was in . . . in . . . in th-th-that c-c-car w-w-w-which j-j-just papa-papa-passed! . . .
!
!

Yes, I am singing tonight at the Winter Garden in Klow . . . Would you like to hear me now? . . .

I'd love to.

Ah, ♫ my beauty ♪ past compare: these jewels ♫ bright I wear! . . .

Was I ever ♩ ♩ ♩ Margar-i-i-ta?

It's lucky the windows are strong!

Hello? . . . Yes, this is Wizskitotz . . . Ah, it's you Sirov . . . Well? . . . What? . . . Szplug! . . . So it's not your fault? . . . Perhaps you think it's mine, eh? . . . What? . . . If he hadn't stuttered so? . . . If! . . . If! . . . You can get round anything with 'if' . . . I'll telephone to the Chief of Police at Zlip . . . Yes, he's one of us . . . He'll stop him on the road.

Well, how did you like that? . . .

V-very much indeed! . . .

In that case, just to please you I'll sing something else!

‼

ЗЛІП

Where is the boy who is travelling with you? . . .

He got out earlier on. He'd forgotten something at the Coachman's Rest, so he went back . . .

I would have given any excuse to escape!

Meanwhile, in Klow . . .

So, you wish to have access to the Treasure House to examine the national archives? . . . I won't conceal from you that this is a privilege rarely accorded to a foreigner, but since our ambassador has vouched for you, I think His Majesty will look favourably upon your request.

That's him . . . We'll ask for his papers . . .

Your papers are not in order! . . . Come with us to the police station!

Quite correct: your papers are not in order! . . . I shall have to keep you here until I receive instructions.

But Captain, there must be some mistake! . . . My passport was stamped before I left and . . .

I am sorry, but I cannot allow you to proceed. Take him away!

!

Captain! . . . You must listen! . . . I have something important to tell you! . . . I . . .

Hello? . . . Wizskitotz? . . . This is Szplodj . . . I've got our fine bird! . . . Yes, we simply picked him up . . . Now what do you want us to do with him? . . . Yes . . . Yes . . . He obviously mustn't get to Klow . . . I'll think it over . . . That's it, ring up in the morning . . . Goodbye . . .

While I cool my heels here, goodness knows what's going on in Klow . . .

Aaaouaaah! . . . It's getting dark . . . I'd better try and get some sleep, as there's nothing else to do . . .

This is Radio Klow . . . We are now broadcasting a concert from the Winter Garden at Klow. The soloist is Signora Bianca Castafiore of La Scala, Milan.

♪♫♪ ♪ # ★ ♩ ♪

Ah, my beauty ♪ past compare; these jewels bright I wear! ♪ ♪ Was I ever Margarita?

Is it I? ♪ Come reply! ♪ Mirror, mirror tell me truly! ♩

Next day . . .

This document bearing the royal signature will admit you to the Treasure Chamber. Lieutenant Kromir will escort you there . . .

The regalia is housed in the keep of Kropow Castle. A special guard is mounted over it.

In the name of the King!

Professor, please come with me.

The regalia seems well guarded!

It is! The man who is clever enough to steal it hasn't been born!

There is His Majesty's regalia, Professor! . . .

And this is the Muniments Room, which adjoins the Treasure Chamber. You must forgive me, but two guards will remain with you for as long as you are here. The doors will also be locked from the outside. Those are the orders. I hope you will not be offended.

Not in the least . . .

Meanwhile . . .

You are to take this young man to Klow. But be careful! . . . He is a dangerous ruffian who has been meddling in State secrets . . . In fact, I've been given to understand, on high authority, that it'd be a good thing if he never arrived in   Klow.

These are your orders . . . You, as the driver, will stage a breakdown. You will get out to look at the engine, and the others will follow . . . The prisoner will then try to escape and . . . You understand me?

Yes, sir! . . . But what if he doesn't try to get away?

Don't worry! . . . He will! . . .

I wonder who can have sent me this? . . . A friend? . . . What friend?

BEWARE! YOU ARE GOING TO BE TAKEN TO KLOW TO BE SHOT! YOU MUST TRY TO ESCAPE. ON THE JOURNEY, PRETEND TO BE ASLEEP. THE DRIVER, WHO IS A FRIEND, WILL STAGE A BREAKDOWN AND CALL THE OTHER GUARDS AWAY. THAT WILL BE THE MOMENT FOR YOU TO MAKE YOUR ESCAPE.

A FRIEND

We'd better get rid of this, in case I'm searched.

Here, Snowy, swallow this paper pellet for me . . .

Hurry up now, Snowy, I think someone is coming for us . . .

I suppose you think it's easy?

Why have you stopped? . . .

It's the engine . . .

Let's have a look . . . Oh, it's all right: he's asleep . . .

Look out, he's moving! . . . He's getting out . . . Get ready . . .

A trap! . . . I'm done for!

There he goes! . . . Don't miss! . . .

There's only one way: a nose-dive! . . . Whoops!

BANG
BANG
BANG

WHIZZ

BANG

WHIZZZ

CRACK

It's no good, hold your fire! . . . He's disappeared behind the boulders! . . . He must have broken his neck . . . but we'd better look for him . . .

He fell down there... Somewhere behind those rocks...

They're coming!...

Careful! About here...

Szplug! Where is he? We've simply got to find him... The captain will never forgive us if we let him get away, after he'd planned that trap...

Come on, let's have another look. He can't be far away...

Whew!... They've passed us...

Now, off we go to Klow!...

I must watch my step!... I see that no one can be trusted!... I must warn the King himself.

Meanwhile in Klow....

I wonder if I might be permitted to photograph some of the documents?

As a rule that is not allowed, but His Majesty might consent...

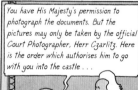
Ah! Here's the main road again.

Golly, I'm hungry...

You have His Majesty's permission to photograph the documents. But the pictures may only be taken by the official Court Photographer, Herr Czarlitz. Here is the order which authorises him to go with you into the castle...

Klow at last!...

When are we going to eat?

Which way to the palace, please?

Follow this street to Ottokar Square, then turn left...

DANGER HIGH VOLTAGE

What a downpour! We'll shelter until this is over...

Is this a restaurant?

It's stopping now . . .

Come on Snowy! . . . We must hurry to warn the King of the danger he's in . . .

Hurry up, Snowy! Hey, where is Snowy?

Snowy! . . . Snowy! . . . Snowy! . . .

They have wonderful bones in this country, Tintin! . . .

?

?

DIPLODOCUS GIGANTICUS

You take that bone back where you found it, at once! You understand . . . And be quick! . . .

Ah! There's the palace!

Could His Majesty grant me an audience? . . . I have most important and urgent business . . .

Please wait here: I will see if His Majesty's aide-de-camp will see you. Whom shall I announce? . . .

Tintin.

Mr Tintin? . . . On important business? . . . All right, show him in.

Certainly, Signora . . . Yes . . . yes . . . tonight, at half past eight . . . His Majesty will be delighted . . . Your servant, Signora . . .

Meanwhile . . .

So that's all arranged, Herr Czarlitz . . . I will come and fetch you in the morning at about nine, and we will go to Kropow Castle together . . .

Very good, Professor.

So you want an audience with His Majesty? . . . May I ask why? . . .

Er . . . I . . . you must excuse me, but . . . it is highly confidential . . .

Sir, I am His Majesty's aide-de-camp! . . . I venture to say that my sovereign places complete trust in me!

I do not doubt it, Colonel! . . . But the news I have to communicate to the King is so serious that it is for his ears alone.

Very well, I will not insist . . . Will you come back tonight, at about half past eight? I will try and arrange for His Majesty to allow you a few minutes, before his reception at the palace . . .

Thank you very much.

Now for a meal, Snowy!

Hello? . . . Yes, this is the Central Committee. Ah, it's you, Boris. What's the latest news? . . . Yes . . . What? . . . Tintin? . . . Are you sure? But the Chief of Police at Zlip has just sworn that . . . Yes . . . Terribly important information.

But he didn't say what it was? . . . Good! . . . Aha! . . . He'll be back tonight at eight-thirty? . . . That's fine, it gives us time . . . Listen, he must not speak to the King . . . Definitely not! . . . This is what we'll do: listen . . .

That evening . . .

The King is willing to grant you a short interview. Please go with the Captain of the Guard and he will take you to the Audience Chamber. His Majesty will see you there.

Thank you.

Ssh! . . . Here they come . . .

Wooah! Wooah!

?

That mongrel has given us away! . . . Come on! . . .

An ambush! . . .

Got you, my friend. Don't try to resist! . . .

!

Traitor! . . .

BONK

Thanks, Snowy.

That's knocked out all four! Fine! Now, let's try and see the King . . .

He should be in here . . .

?

Ah, my beauty past 🎵 compare; ♪ these jewels bright I wear ♪ ♪

CRASH

Quick, it came from the conservatory, outside the Audience Chamber.

The Guard! . . . There isn't a minute to lose! . . .

Let me go! . . . Let me go! . . . I must speak to the King! . . .

Your Majesty! Take care! . . . Don't trust the prof . . .

The Guard! . . . Call the Guard! . . . Hurry!

. . . It was only a young anarchist who managed to get into the palace, Sire . . .

Next morning . . .

More time wasted! . . . And I'm sure the conspirators won't be wasting theirs! . . .

CLINK CLINK CLINK

You are being transferred to the State Prison to await trial. Come with us. The police van is outside . . .

Hello, this is St. Vladimir's Hospital . . . An accident? . . . Casualties? In Moltus Street? . . . All right, I'll send an ambulance.

This one still hasn't come round . . .

Yes, definitely suffering from concussion . . .

We'd better go back for the others . . .

A very useful thing, concussion . . . Come on, Snowy! Now or never . . .

Aha! That's done the trick! . . . Now back to the palace!

I must see the King at all costs.

This time nothing is going to stop me speaking to him! . . .

You aren't hurt, I hope?

No, thank you. I'm all right . . . Great snakes! . . . The King!

Take care, Sire! . . . This is the young anarchist who tried . . .

?

Don't shoot, Sir! . . . Please listen! . . . I am not an anarchist. I wanted to warn you . . . Even at this moment those scoundrels may be trying to steal your sceptre!

What do you mean?

It's the truth, Sir. I am certain that Professor Alembick is an impostor. Coming to Syldavia to study the archives was only a blind. He and his accomplices plan to steal King Ottokar's sceptre, and so force you to give up your throne!

By Vladi-mir! Can it be?

Meanwhile . . .

And this man is in with them, Sir . . . That is why he tried to stop me speaking to you! . . .

It's a lie, Sire!

He's in the plot too?

He is lying, Sire, and I will . . .

You will return to the palace at once and await my orders! . . . I myself will go to Kropow Castle with this young man and prove for myself the truth of his allegations! . . .

We must hurry, Sir . . . I'm sure there's not a moment to lose . . .

That's that . . . May we now go into the Treasure Chamber, and photograph the crown and sceptre? . . .

Certainly.

The light is not very good. We'll have to use a flash-bulb . . .

We're nearly there . . . Those are the towers of Kropow Castle . . . the sceptre is in the keep, that square tower in the centre . . . I only hope we're not too late! . . .

The King! . . .

Everything seems quite normal . . . We are in time!

I hope so, Sir . . .

Where is Professor Alembick?

In the Treasure Chamber, Sire, with the Governor of the Castle and Herr Czarlitz . . .

Open up! In the name of the King!

No answer! Quick, bring me the other keys!

Could it really be possible?

Let us hope not, Sir . . . Ah! Here is the guard with the keys.

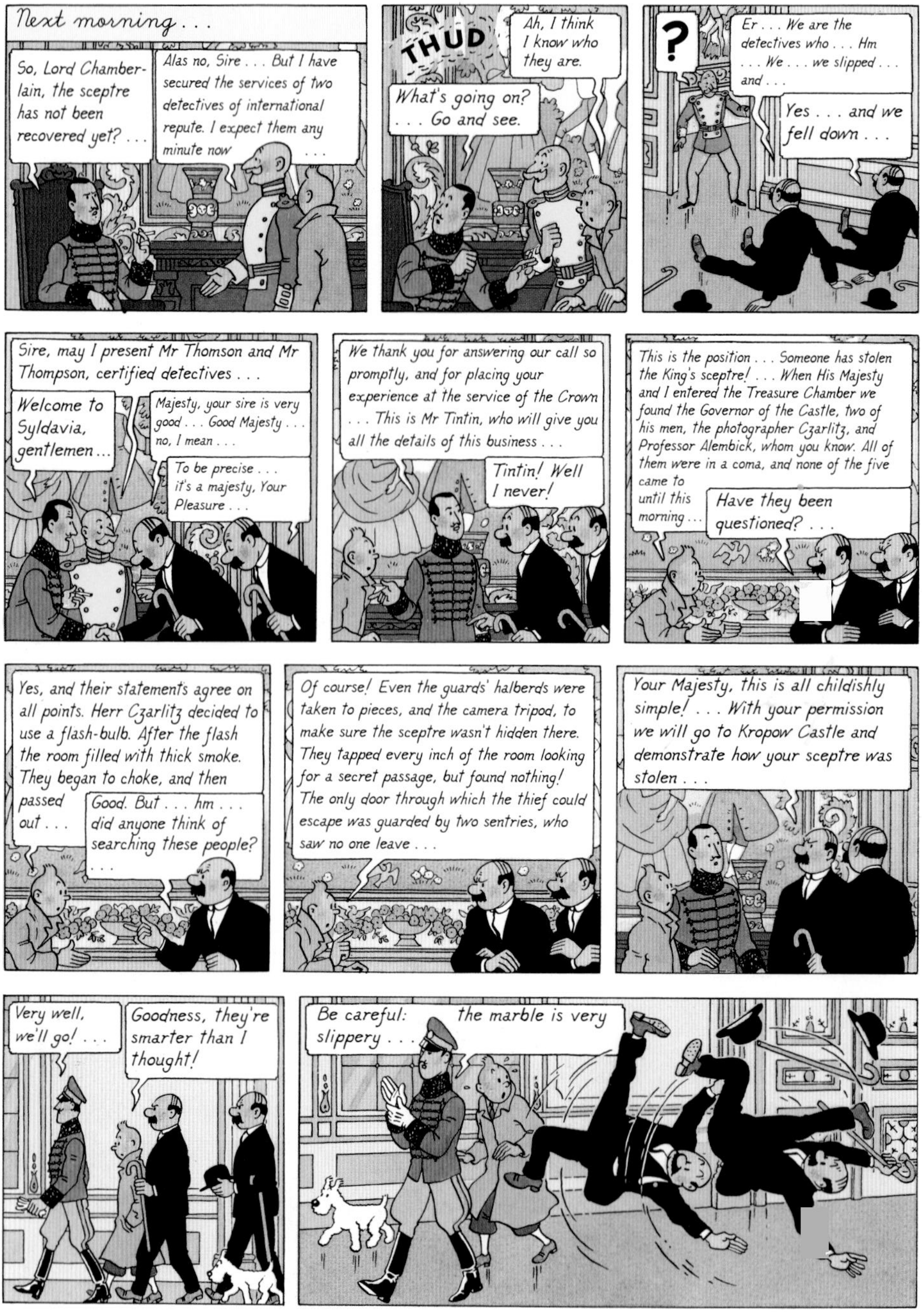

Next morning . . .
So, Lord Chamberlain, the sceptre has not been recovered yet? . . .
Alas no, Sire . . . But I have secured the services of two detectives of international repute. I expect them any minute now . . .
THUD
Ah, I think I know who they are.
What's going on? . . . Go and see.
?
Er . . . We are the detectives who . . . Hm . . . We . . . we slipped . . . and . . .
Yes . . . and we fell down . . .
Sire, may I present Mr Thomson and Mr Thompson, certified detectives . . .
Welcome to Syldavia, gentlemen . . .
Majesty, your sire is very good . . . Good Majesty . . . no, I mean . . .
To be precise . . . it's a majesty, Your Pleasure . . .
We thank you for answering our call so promptly, and for placing your experience at the service of the Crown . . . This is Mr Tintin, who will give you all the details of this business . . .
Tintin! Well I never!
This is the position . . . Someone has stolen the King's sceptre! . . . When His Majesty and I entered the Treasure Chamber we found the Governor of the Castle, two of his men, the photographer Czarlitz, and Professor Alembick, whom you know. All of them were in a coma, and none of the five came to until this morning . . .
Have they been questioned? . . .
Yes, and their statements agree on all points. Herr Czarlitz decided to use a flash-bulb. After the flash the room filled with thick smoke. They began to choke, and then passed out . . .
Good. But . . . hm . . . did anyone think of searching these people? . . .
Of course! Even the guards' halberds were taken to pieces, and the camera tripod, to make sure the sceptre wasn't hidden there. They tapped every inch of the room looking for a secret passage, but found nothing! The only door through which the thief could escape was guarded by two sentries, who saw no one leave . . .
Your Majesty, this is all childishly simple! . . . With your permission we will go to Kropow Castle and demonstrate how your sceptre was stolen . . .
Very well, we'll go! . . .
Goodness, they're smarter than I thought!
Be careful: the marble is very slippery . . .

This is the Treasure Chamber. The sceptre was here . . .

As we said, Your Majesty: the whole thing is childishly simple!

This is what happened. One of the five people present was in the plot. He collapsed when the smoke was released, but took care to hold a handkerchief to his nose. When he was sure the others had been put to sleep he got up, opened the glass case, seized the sceptre, opened the window and dropped the sceptre into the courtyard. There an accomplice collected it, took it away, and that was that!

Impossible, gentlemen! The courtyard is guarded. No one goes there but the sentries; and the sentries are above suspicion . . . They are men of absolute trust who would die rather than betray their King!

As a matter of fact the guard patrolling this side of the tower did hear a window open and shut. But he did not notice anything unusual . . .

Exactly! . . . Because the thief must have thrown the sceptre over the ramparts surrounding the castle! . . . An accomplice waited there, picked it up, and made off.

However, you shall see . . . Could you get me something the same size as the sceptre? . . .

Certainly . . .

But look! It is at least a hundred yards from this window to the ramparts! . . . And there are bars . . .

What do they matter? . . . It just needs a good aim . . .

There . . . Will this do? . . .

Perfectly.

Now I'll show you . . .

? BONG

Clumsy oaf! . . . Let me show you the right way to do it! . . .

Watch carefully! . . .

BONG ?

You can see for yourselves that the sceptre didn't leave this room like that! . . .

Yes . . . Yes . . . maybe. Anyway, we'd like to question Alembick and Czarlitz . . .

Sire! . . . Sire! . . . Ah, at last I've found you . . .

Sire! . . . It's unbelievable! . . . Professor Alembick and Herr Czarlitz . . .

. . . have escaped from the State Prison, Sire . . . They had accomplices among the warders! . . . Four of them have disappeared with the fugitives!

By the Sceptre of Ottokar!

Accomplices! . . . Accomplices! . . . They are everywhere! . . . Oh, this plot was well laid: all is lost!

Leave it to us, Your Majesty . . . It may take a week, a month, even a year, but we will recover your sceptre! . . .

Alas, gentlemen, there are only three days! . . . If I am without my sceptre on St. Vladimir's Day, I have no choice but to abdicate!

'Only three days', said Columbus, 'and I will give you a new world!' Only three days, Majesty, and we swear to bring your sceptre, bound hand and foot . . .

Thank you, gentlemen! May you succeed.

This time our honour is at stake! We have sworn to find the sceptre; we must keep our word!

To be precise: we must keep our word!

St. Vladimir protect them! . . . They will succeed, won't they? . . .

I hope so, Sir, with all my heart!

In any case, I'd like your permission to try to solve this mystery myself.

Thank you, my friend. Whatever happens, I shall never forget what you have done for me!

The vital thing is to find out HOW the sceptre was stolen . . .

TC

YS

⁉ ⚡ !

Eureka! . . . Eureka! . . . I've got it!

YS

Quick, back to the castle!

I've got it! . . . Come with me to the Treasure Chamber! . . . I'll show you! . . .

Show me what?

How the sceptre was stolen! . . . Quick! Follow me!

Don't go so fast! . . . Wait for me! . . .

Has he gone in? . . .

Yes, sir . . .

?

OW!

?!

?

111

What happened? . . .
Quick, tell us! . . .

The camera! . . . Look at
the camera! . . .

A spring? . . .

Yes, this spring came out.
It hit me in the face and
knocked me out! . . .

It's amazing! . . . How did you
discover that?

By walking past a toy-shop! . . .
I saw a little spring gun; it gave
me the idea that perhaps the
camera was faked up to hide
a spring capable of throwing
the sceptre beyond the castle
ramparts! And my guess
was right! . . .

Watch! . . . There's the spring back in
place . . . I insert into the tube this
stick used by the two detectives . . .

I place the camera by the window,
the forked end of our makeshift
sceptre through the bars . . .

I click the shutter,
and . . . Whoops!

It's fallen in the wood, beyond
the river! . . . I'm going to have
a look round over there.

You will find a boat
down by the bank . . .

?

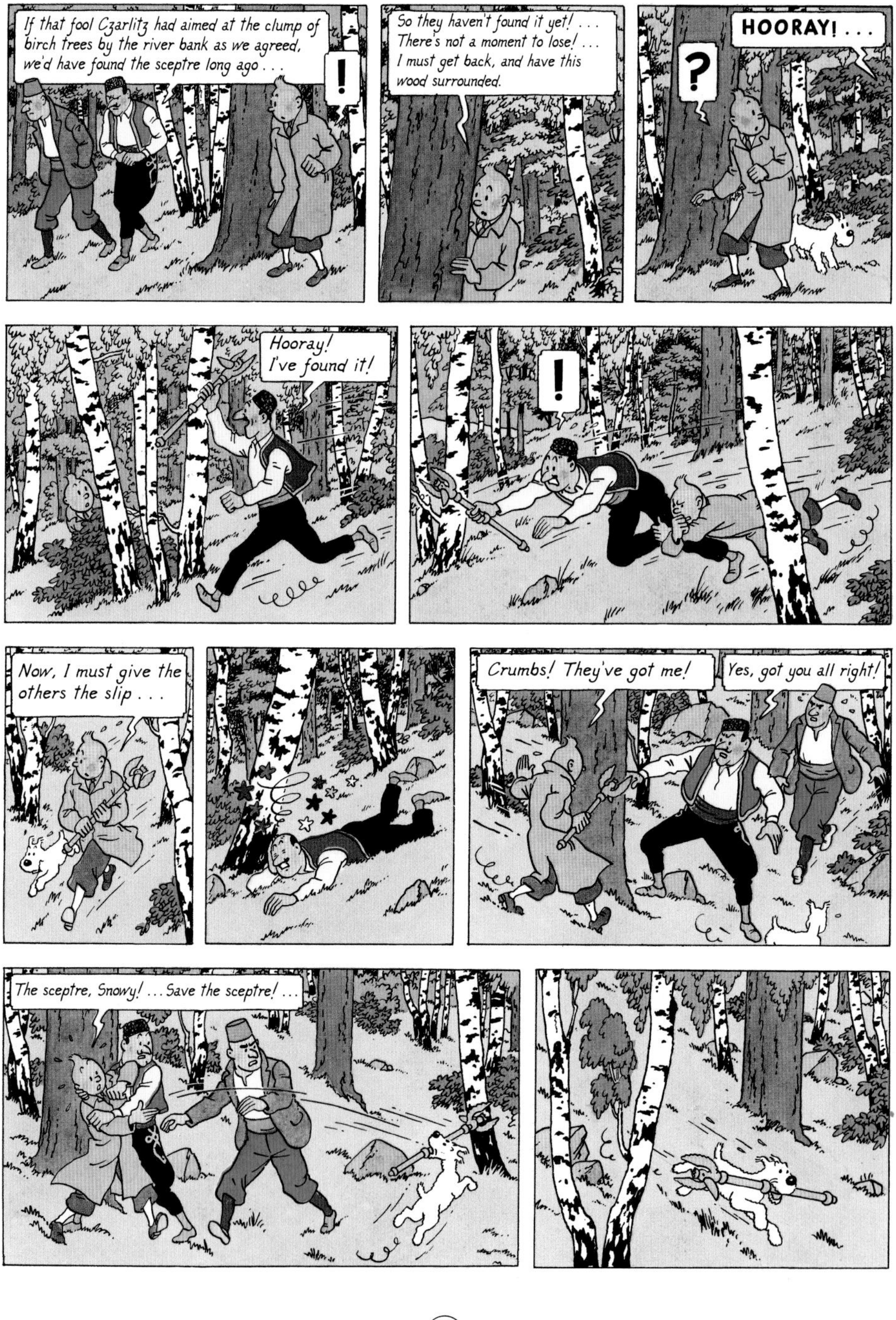
If that fool Czarlitz had aimed at the clump of birch trees by the river bank as we agreed, we'd have found the sceptre long ago . . .
!
So they haven't found it yet! . . . There's not a moment to lose! . . . I must get back, and have this wood surrounded.
?
HOORAY! . . .
Hooray! I've found it!
!
Now, I must give the others the slip . . .
Crumbs! They've got me!
Yes, got you all right!
The sceptre, Snowy! . . . Save the sceptre! . . .

Come here, you mangy cur! ... Come here!

Here's the river! ... In we go! ... Just let them try and catch me!

?

!

BANG
BANG

Every man for himself, boys! ... The police! ...

Poor old Tintin!

Where's the sceptre? They've got it again! ... Snowy dropped it!

Too late!

How did you know I was here?

When we went back to the castle they told us you had crossed the river . . .

There's the King . . . They told him, too. He went round by the bridge while we crossed in a boat . . .

Well, what has happened? . . .

Those gangsters have got away in a car, with the sceptre! . . . If you will lend us your car, Sir, we three will try and catch them . . .

They haven't got much of a start on us . . . We'll soon catch them up.

We're almost out of petrol . . . We'll have to stop at the first pump we come to . . .

Ah! There's one . . .

. . Five gallons! . . . And make it snappy! . . .

Another twenty miles to the frontier . . . Good! . . . In half an hour we shall be clear of Syldavia, and the sceptre will be safe!

The King's car! . . . They're after us!

We certainly caught them on the hop! ... They've taken to the mountains!

They hadn't even time to get back into their car ...

We must hurry! ... They mustn't get away!

They're still following us ...

We must stop this! ... We'll fool them! ...

Come on! ... We'll get them! ...

BANG

Take cover everybody ... They are shooting at us!

BANG

Where have Thomson and Thompson got to? ... I can't see them anywhere.

BANG

CRACK

There must be some way of catching them ...

Follow me, Snowy, and don't show yourself! ... We'll sneak round behind them.

Hello, where's the third one? . . .

Not a sign of life . . .

Perhaps we hit him . . . Look! There are the other two . . .

Hands up!

Now, I see! . . . You blocked our way while your pal got away with the sceptre! . . .

Quick! You look after these thugs! . . . I'm going on . . .

Szplug! I can't understand it . . . He's still on my tail! . . .

It's getting dark . . . We can't keep this up much longer.

We can't go on now . . . We'll have to spend the night here! . . .

We can only wait until it's light . . .

Next day, at dawn . . .

Off we go Snowy! . . . We simply must recover the sceptre!

We'll walk fast: That will warm us up . . .

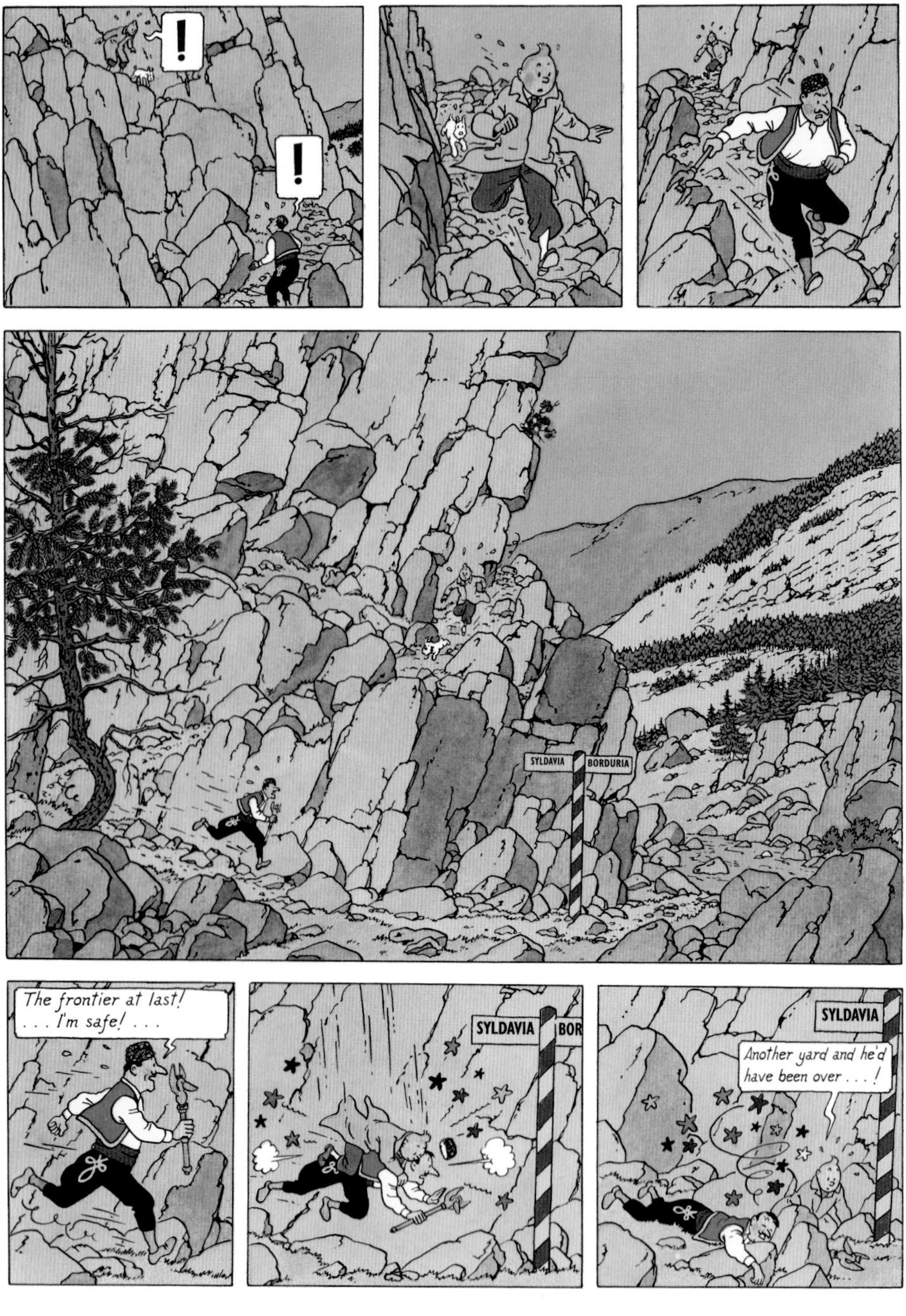
!
!
SYLDAVIA
BORDURIA
The frontier at last! . . . I'm safe! . . .
SYLDAVIA
BOR
SYLDAVIA
Another yard and he'd have been over . . . !

One day you'll break your neck with all those acrobatics! . . .

Let's search him . . . Ah! Here's his wallet . . .

?

Z.Z.R.K.   1239
SECRET   To Section Commanders, Shock Troops
SUBJECT: Seizure of Power
I wish to draw your attention to the order in which the operations for seizure of power in Syldavia will take place.
On the eve of St Vladimir's Day, agents in our propaganda units will foment incidents, and arrange for Bordurian nationals to be beaten up.
On St Vladimir's Day, at 12 o'clock (H-hour), shock troops will seize Radio Klow, the airfield, the gas works and power station, the banks, the general post office, the Royal Palace, Kropow Castle, etc. . . .
In due course each section commander will receive precise orders concerning his particular mission.
I salute you!
(signed)
Müsstler.

Z.Z.R.K.   1240
SECRET   To Section Commanders, Shock Troops
SUBJECT: Seizure of Power
I wish to remind you that I shall broadcast a call to arms when Radio Klow is in our hands.
Motorized Bordurian troops will then cross into Syldavian territory, to free our native land from the tyranny of King Muskar XII.
Allowing for the feeble resistance they may meet with from a few fanatical royalist partisans and certain subversive sections of the populace, the Bordurian troops will arrive in Klow at about 5.00 p.m.
I call upon all members of Z.Z.R.K. to defend until then, with the last drop of their blood, the positions they will have occupied at midday.
I salute you!
(signed)
Müsstler.

There's no time to lose! We must get back to Klow as fast as we can . . .

Not on foot I hope?

What's the matter with me?

Oh, I know . . . I haven't eaten anything since yesterday! If only I had some food!

There's a house over there . . . But it's across the frontier. Can't be helped . . . I'm too hungry!

A Bordurian frontier post! . . .

Crumbs! He's come to . . .
I'm cut off!

BANG

WOOF
WOOF

He's a dangerous Syldavian spy!
. . .We must capture him! . . .

Look out! He may
be hiding in that
house . . .

No, he's gone
. . . Come on!

What's the matter with him?

SNIFF

What's he
sniffing at? . . .

SNIFF
SNIFF

SNIFF

Pep . . . Tchoo! . . .
It's pepper . . . Aaaa
. . . tchoo!

Little devil! He's scattered
pepper to put the dog off
the scent!

Next day...

That's two nights in the open ... I'm tired out! ... If I don't find the way soon I'll never get back in time!

A Bordurian fighter!

He's lowered his undercarriage... Where's he landing?

If I could grab one of those planes I'd be in Klow in less than an hour...

Everything OK?

Yes, nothing unusual ... just reconnaissance along the frontier...

You know, I've been tipped off that Müsstler will give his broadcast at midday tomorrow ... And an hour later our squadron will land at Klow.

?!★©!★!

Flat out for Klow! ...

It's getting dark ... That's annoying. I shan't be there before nightfall ...

Hello? Ack-Ack H.Q.? ... This is Listening Post 34 ... A Bordurian aircraft has crossed the frontier, heading for Klow ... What shall we do?

You have your orders, Lieutenant. Shoot it down! ...

121

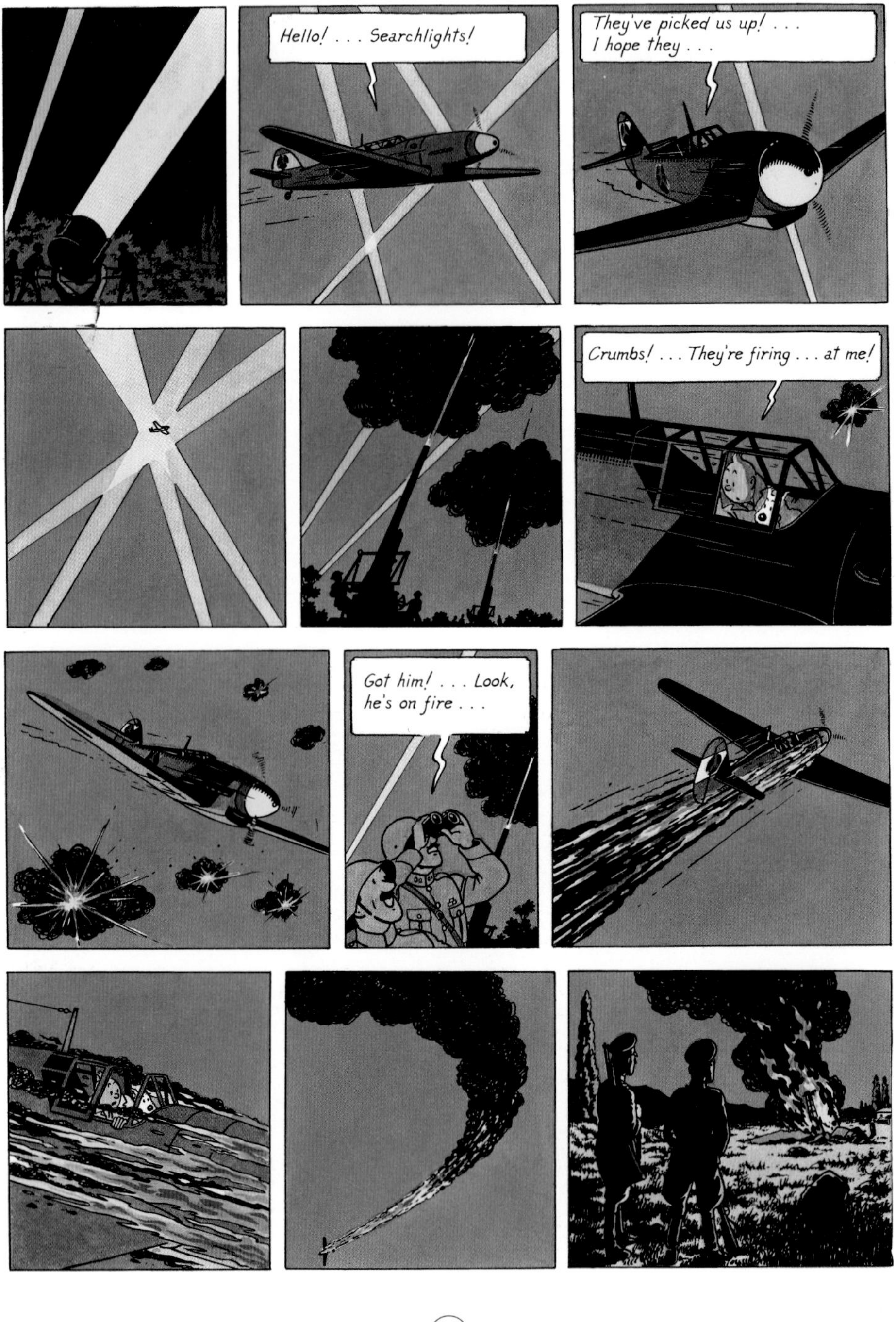
Hello! . . . Searchlights!
They've picked us up! . . . I hope they . . .
Crumbs! . . . They're firing . . . at me!
Got him! . . . Look, he's on fire . . .

Ah, a signpost! . . .
That's a stroke of luck!

ISTOW
19½ miles

KLOW
15¾ miles

Sixteen miles:
that's five
hours' walk! . . .

A mere
trifle!

A farm! . . . Stables!
. . . If only I could
borrow a horse . . .

That's a
splendid
idea!

Aha, here's a horse! . . .
Whoa there! . . . Good, here's
a saddle too . . . Whoa now!
Gently does it . . .

On the whole I think we'd
better go on foot.

Why not? . . . A little
walk will do us good.

That night . . .

Things are grave,
Sire! . . . the people
are suspicious: there
are rumours that the
sceptre is missing.
Furthermore . . .

. . . Bordurian shops were looted again
yesterday. These incidents are of course
the work of agitators in the pay of a foreign
power, but we are faced with a dangerous
situation. And if Your Majesty appears before
the crowds without the sceptre, I fear . . .

Rest assured, Prime Minister,
there will be no bloodshed. I will
abdicate.

No, Sir, you will not
abdicate . . .

! TINTIN! ?

Your Majesty, I have your
sceptre with me now!

Saved!

Here it is! . . . I . . . Great
snakes! I've lost it on the way!

Lucky I saw the sceptre fall out of his pocket!

!

???

Saved! . . . I am saved! . . . How happy this makes me!

Saved for the moment only, Sir. I have discovered something else . . .

I found these on the ruffians I went after.

'Seizure of power'! . . . And it's signed Müsstler . . . Müsstler, the leader of the Iron Guard!

Not a moment to lose! Arrest Müsstler and his associates at once!

Yes, Sire! . . .

General, the review of the army will not take place tomorrow as arranged. By 8 a.m., crack regiments will occupy defensive positions along the frontier. And take over all the strategic points which the rebels plan to attack . . .

Very good, Sire!

Some hours later . . .

COCKADOODLEDOO

BOOM

BOOM

Guns! . . .

Come in!

RAT
TAT
TAT

Oh, it's you! ... What is all that firing for?

That? ...

They are firing a salute for St. Vladimir's Day ... Hurry up and dress, or we shall miss the procession.

And so the royal carriage leaves the palace ... the King, smiling, bare-headed, is holding the sceptre of Ottokar in his hand ... A great roar of welcome greets His Majesty, a roar which fades only when the strains of our national anthem swell from a thousand voices ...

And now the King is once more in his palace. Time and again the delirious crowds have called His Majesty back on to the balcony to receive their tumultuous acclaim. But now he is seated here in the Throne Room, where an investiture is taking place ...

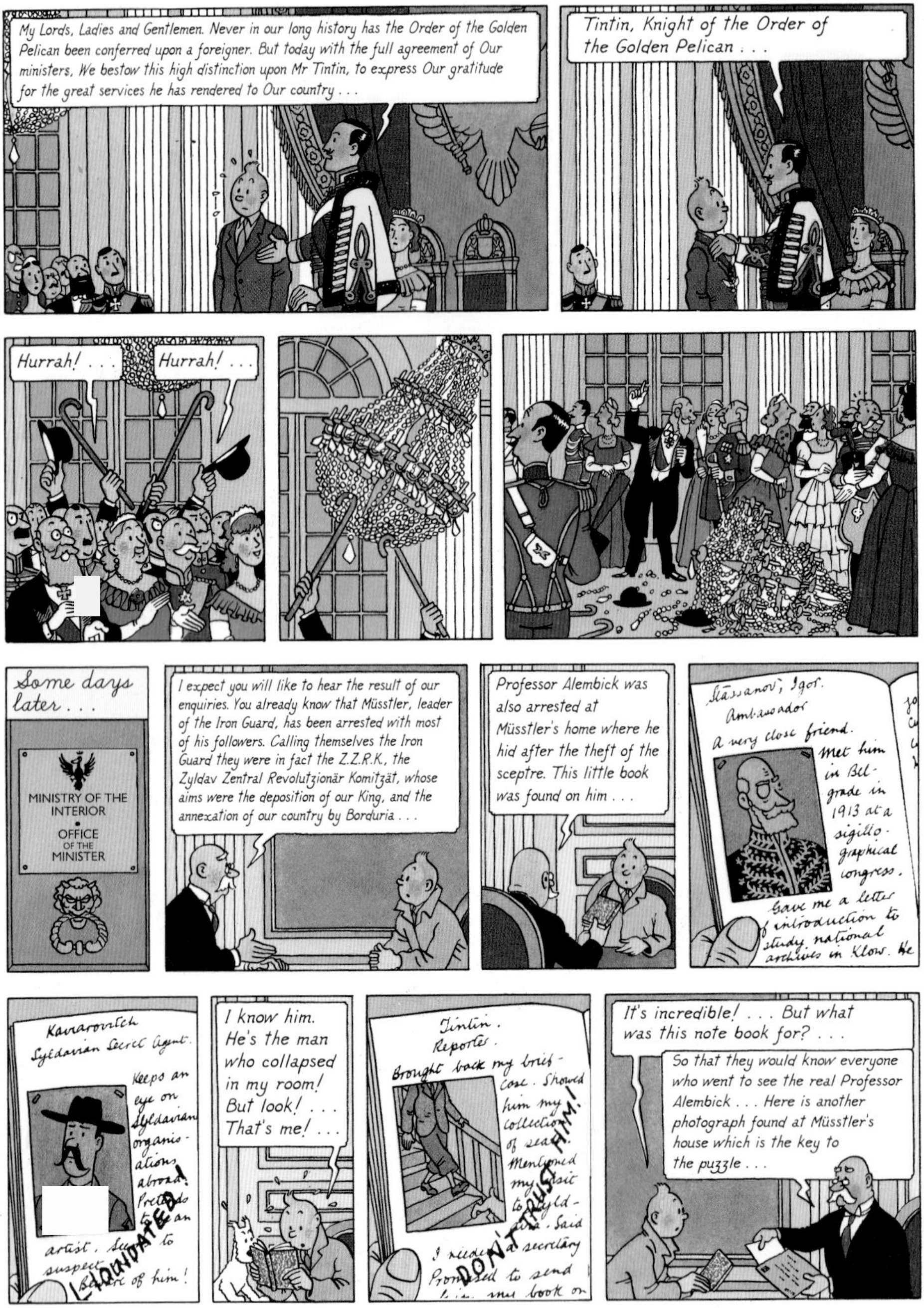
My Lords, Ladies and Gentlemen. Never in our long history has the Order of the Golden Pelican been conferred upon a foreigner. But today with the full agreement of Our ministers, We bestow this high distinction upon Mr Tintin, to express Our gratitude for the great services he has rendered to Our country . . .
Tintin, Knight of the Order of the Golden Pelican . . .
Hurrah! . . .
Hurrah! . . .
Some days later . . .
MINISTRY OF THE INTERIOR
OFFICE OF THE MINISTER
I expect you will like to hear the result of our enquiries. You already know that Müsstler, leader of the Iron Guard, has been arrested with most of his followers. Calling themselves the Iron Guard they were in fact the Z.Z.R.K., the Zyldav Zentral Revolutzionär Komitzät, whose aims were the deposition of our King, and the annexation of our country by Borduria . . .
Professor Alembick was also arrested at Müsstler's home where he hid after the theft of the sceptre. This little book was found on him . . .
Ambassador
A very close friend.
Met him in Belgrade in 1913 at a sigillographical congress.
Gave me a letter of introduction to study national archives in Klow. He
Syldavian Secret Agent.
Keeps an eye on Syldavian organisations abroad!
artist.
suspect
of him!
LIQUIDATED
I know him. He's the man who collapsed in my room! But look! . . . That's me! . . .
Tintin.
Reporter.
Brought back my brief-case. Showed him my collection
DON'T TRUST HIM!
a secretary
book on
It's incredible! . . . But what was this note book for? . . .
So that they would know everyone who went to see the real Professor Alembick . . . Here is another photograph found at Müsstler's house which is the key to the puzzle . . .

Twins! ... I might have guessed it! ...
But what happened to the real professor? ...

Well, I've just read the London newspapers. Listen: 'During a search carried out yesterday in a house occupied by Syldavian nationals, the police found Professor Alembick, the scholar. He had been imprisoned in a cellar for some weeks. He said he had been kidnapped on the eve of his departure for Syldavia, and his passport was taken...'

Now I see it all! First the shouts on the telephone; then the professor not wearing his glasses, and not smoking any more... It explains everything.

Meanwhile at Bordurian military headquarters...

... to prove our peaceful intentions, despite the inexplicable attitude of the Syldavians, I have ordered our troops to withdraw fifteen miles from the frontier ...

Next day...

In a private audience this morning the King received Mr Tintin, Mr Thomson and Mr Thompson, who paid their respects before leaving Syldavia. Afterwards the party left by road for Douma, where they embarked in a flying boat of the regular Douma-Southampton service...

RADIO KLOW
SZCHT-SILENCE

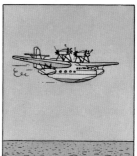

Some hours later...

Ten past six.
We're there...

Goodness, what on earth's happening? ...

We're falling into the sea ...

We aren't FALLING: we're landing! This is a flying-boat, remember!

? ?

How absurd! . . . I had completely forgotten!

Me too! . . . That was a good joke!

Isn't it amazing how absent-minded one can be! . . .

Quite absurd!

I can still hear you shouting: 'We're falling into the sea'!

Ha Ha! Ha Ha! Ha Ha!

HERGÉ
★
THE ADVENTURES OF
TINTIN
★
THE CRAB
WITH
THE GOLDEN CLAWS

EGMONT

THE CRAB
WITH
THE G⊕LDEN CLAWS

Yow! . . . ow! . . . ow!

?

There you are, Snowy. You see what comes of your dirty habit of exploring rubbish bins . . . I don't go scavenging, do I?

You've been lucky! You could have cut yourself. Look how jagged the edges are.

Now, come on! . . . And don't do that again, or I'll buy a muzzle and you'll walk on a lead!

Hi! Hello there, Tintin!

OLYMPIA BA

Waiter, bring another drink!

Yes, sir.

My dear Tintin, how nice to see you again! . . .

To be precise: how nice to see you again, my dear Tintin!

Here you are, sir.

Your health!

And yours!

My dear old friends, how nice to see you again!

Well, now, what's going on?

Everything's fine: we've just been entrusted with a very important case.

Oh? . . .

To be precise: a very . . . er . . . important case.

Oh? . . .

Look . . . Have you read this?

"Watch out for counterfeit coins!" . . . Yes, I saw it.

Well, we two have been instructed to clear this thing up.

Oh? . . . Jolly good! . . . I say, is it easy to spot one of these fakes?

Oh, you know how it is. People like ourselves who have examined them can tell one in a flash, of course . . .

Waiter! . . . How much?

Forty-five pence, sir.

Here's fifty pence! . . . But most people are easily fooled by them.

I'm sorry, sir . . .

Good gracious, someone's slipped me a dud fifty-pence piece!

CLUNK

There!

Thank you.

If you've nothing better to do, come along with us. We'll show you the papers we've already collected in our investigations.

Thanks.

Where did you put those papers?

But you put them away yourself!

!

133

What's that?

That? . . . It all came from Police Headquarters. They are things taken from a body found in the sea. Did you notice? He had five coins on him, all duds . . . Odd, don't you think?

Very odd! . . . May I . . . ?

I'll be back in a minute!

I'm going after him!

What's bitten him!

Good gracious! I've forgotten my stick!

Good gracious! He's forgotten his stick!

There he is!

We've caught him up.

What on earth's the matter?...

Well, the scrap of paper among those things found on the drowned man comes from the label off a tin ...

... and I was holding the very tin from which it was torn, just before I met you! Here we are. I threw it into that dustbin ... that one where the tramp is rummaging.

Tintin!... Aren't you ashamed of yourself? Rummaging in dustbins like a common mongrel off the streets!

One moment, please...

It's gone!... Yet I'm sure I threw it there. A tin of crab, I remember quite clearly.

Open your sack!

No, it's not here ...

That's odd; in fact, it's fishy.

To be precise: it's fishy ...

What's all the fuss about?

Those chaps are absolutely daft! They are looking for an empty tin! A crab tin ...

A crab tin! Are they indeed!

Now, let's have a good look at this bit of paper...

Aha! That's interesting! There's something written here in pencil, almost obliterated by the water...

I must look at this through a magnifying glass.

Gnawing a bone again? Where did this one come from?...

Can't you ever do as you're told?

There!... And mind you don't do it again!

Did I leave it in my study?...

It's not here either!

CRASH

?

Crumbs! That made me jump... And it was only the wind slamming the door!

But now I think of it, that bit of paper...

...must have been blown away when I went into my study the first time to get my magnifying glass!

That's the answer. There it is!

Now let's have a look...

Have I gone crazy? I'm positive I put my magnifying glass down here a moment ago!

?

I'll go over all this in pencil. There's 'K'... and an 'A'... and that's an 'R'... or an 'I'... there, I'll soon have it...

Karaboudjan

KARABOUDJAN . . . that's an Armenian name. Karaboudjan . . .

An Armenian name. So . . . now what? . . . That doesn't help me much!

What's going on? . . .

That was my landlady's voice. I must go and see what's happened.

It was a Japanese or a Chinese gentleman with a letter for you, Mr Tintin. But just as he was going to give it to me a car came by, and stopped . . .

. . . outside the door. Three men got out; they attacked the Chinese gentleman and knocked him down! . . . Of course I shouted: 'Help! Help!' but one of the gangsters threatened me with a huge revolver, as big as that! Then they threw the Japanese gentleman into their car and drove off . . . with the letter addressed to you . . .

A tin + a drowned man + five counterfeit coins + Karaboudjan + a Japanese + a letter + a kidnapping = a real Chinese puzzle.

The next morning . . .

RRRING
RRRING
RRRING

Hello? . . . Yes . . . Oh, it's you! . . . What's the news? . . . What? . . .

Yes, the drowned man has been identified: the one who had the mysterious bit of paper and the five dud coins. His name was Herbert Dawes; he was a sailor from the merchant-ship KARABOUDJAN.

The merchant-ship KARABOUDJAN! Did you say KARABOUDJAN?

To the docks, Snowy
. . . as quick as we can!

KARABOUDJAN

79

KARABO

What a
lot of
seagulls!

WHAT THE . . . ?!

Confound it! . . .
Missed him!

Well, Snowy my lad, if I hadn't
happened to be watching the
seagulls we'd have been flattened . . .

What happened? . . .

Oh, it's you! Well, I just missed being squashed by that heavy crate! . . . But what are you doing here?

The chain broke . . .

We are going aboard the KARABOUDJAN to inquire about the sailor who was drowned.

Are you? May I come too? It would give me a chance to look round the ship . . .

Will you be long on board?

No, only about half an hour.

He's coming aboard with the two detectives!

You take care of him, while I talk to them . . . He mustn't go back on shore!

I get it!

All right then? . . . I'll wait for you here in half an hour . . .

Here? . . . Good.

How do you do, Mister Mate. We've come about that unfortunate sailor . . .

I'm at your service, gentlemen. Will you come into my cabin? We can talk more easily there . . .

Mind the step . . .

Yes, I see it.

. . . and the door is a bit low . . .

140

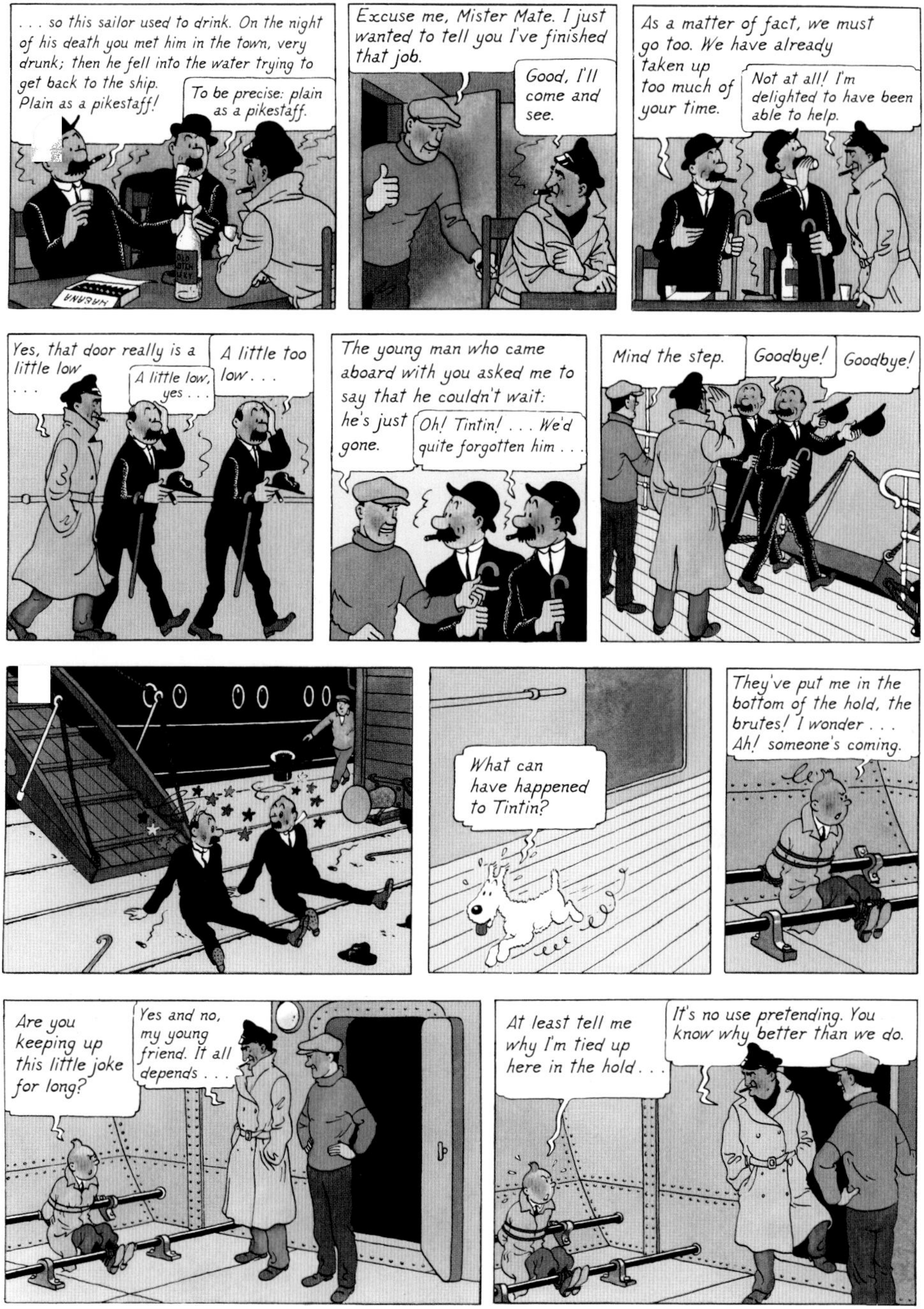
. . . so this sailor used to drink. On the night of his death you met him in the town, very drunk; then he fell into the water trying to get back to the ship. Plain as a pikestaff!
To be precise: plain as a pikestaff.
HAVANA
Excuse me, Mister Mate. I just wanted to tell you I've finished that job.
Good, I'll come and see.
As a matter of fact, we must go too. We have already taken up too much of your time.
Not at all! I'm delighted to have been able to help.
Yes, that door really is a little low . . .
A little low, yes . . .
A little too low . . .
The young man who came aboard with you asked me to say that he couldn't wait: he's just gone.
Oh! Tintin! . . . We'd quite forgotten him . . .
Mind the step.
Goodbye!
Goodbye!
What can have happened to Tintin?
They've put me in the bottom of the hold, the brutes! I wonder . . . Ah! someone's coming.
Are you keeping up this little joke for long?
Yes and no, my young friend. It all depends . . .
At least tell me why I'm tied up here in the hold . . .
It's no use pretending. You know why better than we do.

But . . .

SLAM

Snowy!! Good old Snowy! How did you get in here? . . . It must have been while those two scoundrels . . .

Ssh! . . . Listen . . .

TOOOOOT

We're sailing . . . for an unknown destination. But it's no good rotting away down here. Snowy, bite through these ropes and we'll take the first chance we get to say goodbye to these pirates!

Here's a coded radio message just in from the Boss. Read it . . .

'Send T to the bottom'

And I've just sent Pedro down with some food for him! . . . Oh well! I'll take a rope and a lump of lead, and that'll soon fix him.

It's very kind of you to bring me that, but how am I going to eat with my hands tied behind my back?

You're right, I'll have to loosen them a bit. But mind you, no tricks . . .

. . . make one false move . . . you get me? . . .

?

. . . he asked me to free his hands so he could eat; but as soon as I bent down he hit me a terrific crack . . .

. . . and that's nothing to what the mate will do to you!

Idiot! . . . Nitwit! . . . Now we'll have to find him, you fool!

. . . and now he's got a gun.

I hope these are cases of food. Then we can withstand a siege behind our barricade! Anyway . . .

Let's see . . .

Great snakes! . . . Tins of crab!

No doubt about it, these are the same as the tin we tried to find! . . .

We'll sort that out later. Let's go on checking our stores.

Champagne too! Snowy my boy, our supplies are taken care of!

And how!

Let me offer you a drink, Snowy . . .

Ssh! . . .

Quiet! . . . They're looking for us! They mustn't find us . . .

BANG

It's no good trying to open that door. He'll have barricaded himself in. We'll starve him out: he's nothing to eat . . .

. . . that's what you think, gentlemen!

!?

Opium! . . .

So we've managed to get ourselves mixed up with drug-runners!

This certainly changes everything! They were quite right: we've nothing to eat! . . .

Who cares? We've plenty to drink!

Let's see if we can't get out somehow.

Golly, how she rolls!

No, we can't reach the port-hole above; it's too far . . .

Unless . . . yes, I've got an idea . . .

Meanwhile . . .

Mister Mate, the Captain wants you . . .

The Captain? . . . What does he want, the old drunkard?

Yes, I sent f-f-for you, Mister Mate; it's wicked! I'm . . . it's wicked! . . . I'm being allowed to d-die of thirst! . . . I . . . I haven't a d-d-drop of whisky!

That's quite intolerable, Captain. I'll have some sent in at once.

At any rate, you-you-you are my friend, Mr Allan. You're the only one who . . . one who . . . who . . .

Of course, of course, you know I wouldn't deprive you of whisky for anything in the world . . .

For then I'll be the boss on this ship and do just as I like!

That night . . .

Now it's dark I'll try out my plan.

BONK

?

Let's have another shot.

No one there! But what . . . ?

. . . perhaps it's the whisky . . .

Ssh! . . . Not a sound!

Who-who . . . who are you?

Someone forced to sail in this vile tub and . . .

Vile tub? . . . I . . . d-d-do you know I'm Captain Haddock! And I can have you -y-y-you clapped in irons!

Thanks! I've just got out of them! I've spent enough time in your hold with its cargo of opium!

O-o-opium? There's opium in the hold? . . . In my hold . . . m-m-mine? . . .

Didn't you know?

Opium! . . . But h-h-how? . . . It's frightful! . . . I'm an hon . . . an honest man . . . and not . . . but who . . . ? It must be Allan, the f-first mate, who has . . . he . . . he's double-crossing me . . .

Listen, you must help me. And you must promise to stop drinking. Think of your reputation, Captain! What would your old mother say if she saw you in such a state? . . .

M-m-my old mother? . . .

There, there, Captain! . . .

Boo hoo . . . Boo . . . hoo . . . hoo Booh . . . hoo Booh . . . hoo.

For goodness' sake be quiet . . .

Boo . . . hoo . . . Mummy! M-M-Mummy!

Let's go and see. Perhaps he's gone crazy . . .

Too late! I'm trapped . . .

Mummy . . . Boo . . . hoo . . hoo . . .

What's going on here? . . .

Mummy . . . Boo . . . hoo . . hoo . . .

I'm a miserable wretch . . .

Here, drink this . . . You'll feel better . . .

FFFFH

N-n-no . . . I . . . I promised him not to drink . . . and I won't any more!

Who did you promise that to? . . .

To the y-y-young man who . . . who who . . . who was here . . .

What young man? Answer me!

By thunder!

I don't know . . . I've never seen him before.

The little devil! So he managed to get in here! . . . Luckily that drunken bawling scared him off. But he may try to come back . . .

Jumbo, stay and watch this port-hole. If anyone tries to climb in here, get him. Understand? . . . here's a gun . . .   Right.

We must settle his hash! We'll blow in the door of the hold where he's hiding!

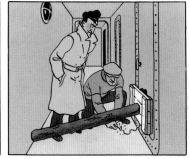

That's it! . . . Take cover . . .

That must have knocked him out . . .   Or else he's shamming . . .

The swine!   BANG

BANG BANG BANG

A champagne cork!   In that case . . .

BANG

147

Quick! Back again! . . .

I watched the port-hole carefully, Mister Mate, but not the locker under the bunk . . . And that's where he was hiding! . . .

Mister Mate, the wireless operator! . . . I just found him, bound and gagged!

It's a rum thing, Mister Mate! . . . The longboat has vanished!

Dawn at last. We're safe for the moment: the KARABOUDJAN has disappeared over the horizon.

But we're not out of trouble yet! We must be sixty miles from the Spanish coast. We must save our energy. You sleep for a bit. Then I'll have a rest while you take a turn at the oars.

OK.

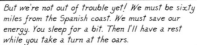

148

Heavens, I'm thirsty! ... And cold! ...

I remember: there's a keg of fresh water here, and biscuits ...

... and some rum!

But I swore never to drink again, and I'll keep my word!

Maybe if I only had a little drop ...

... just to warm myself up?

Aaaah! ... That's the stuff to keep the cold out!

Now, just one more sip ...

and I'll throw it away ...

Hello, it's empty already!

Poor l-l-little chap! He's fast asleep!

But he must be f-f-frightfully c-c-cold, too ...

Aha! I've got an idea ...

!?

Our oars! Hey! . . .
You're burning our oars!
Have you gone mad? . . .

Ah! here's
a bucket!

If . . . if you p-p-put that out . . .
y-you'll have to settle with m-m-me,
you miserable whipper-snapper . . .

Let go of that bucket, you
meddlesome cabin-boy!

?

?

What have I done? Oh, Columbus
. . . What have I done!

You've got us into a fine
mess . . .

I'm sorry . . . I'm sorry! . . . I'm a
miserable wretch . . . I drank the
rum from the locker . . . I'm
sorry! . . .

Ssh! . . .

A seaplane! . . .
We're saved! . . .

It's got Moroccan
markings: CN.

RAT
TAT TAT
TAT
TAT
TAT TAT
TAT
TAT

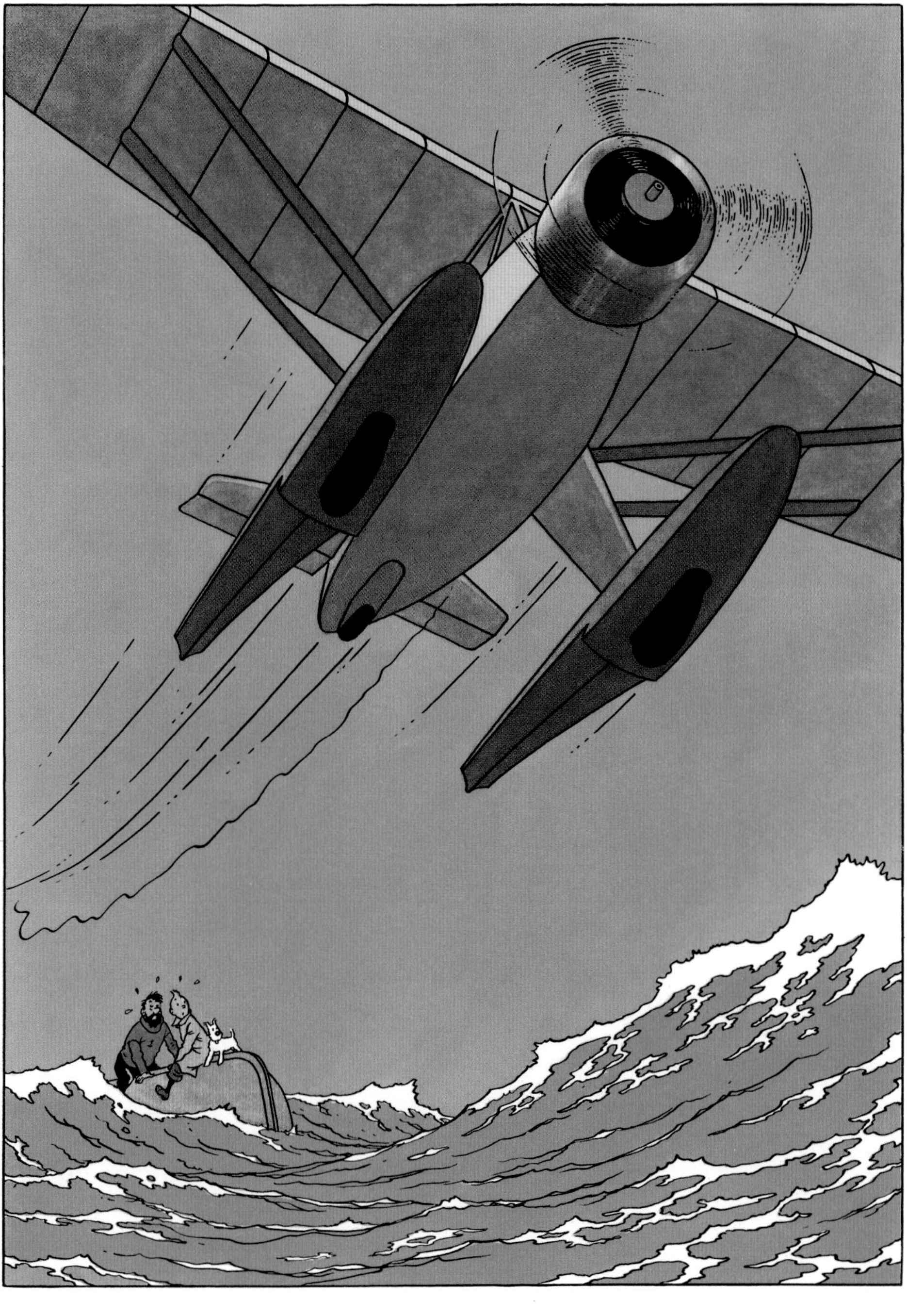

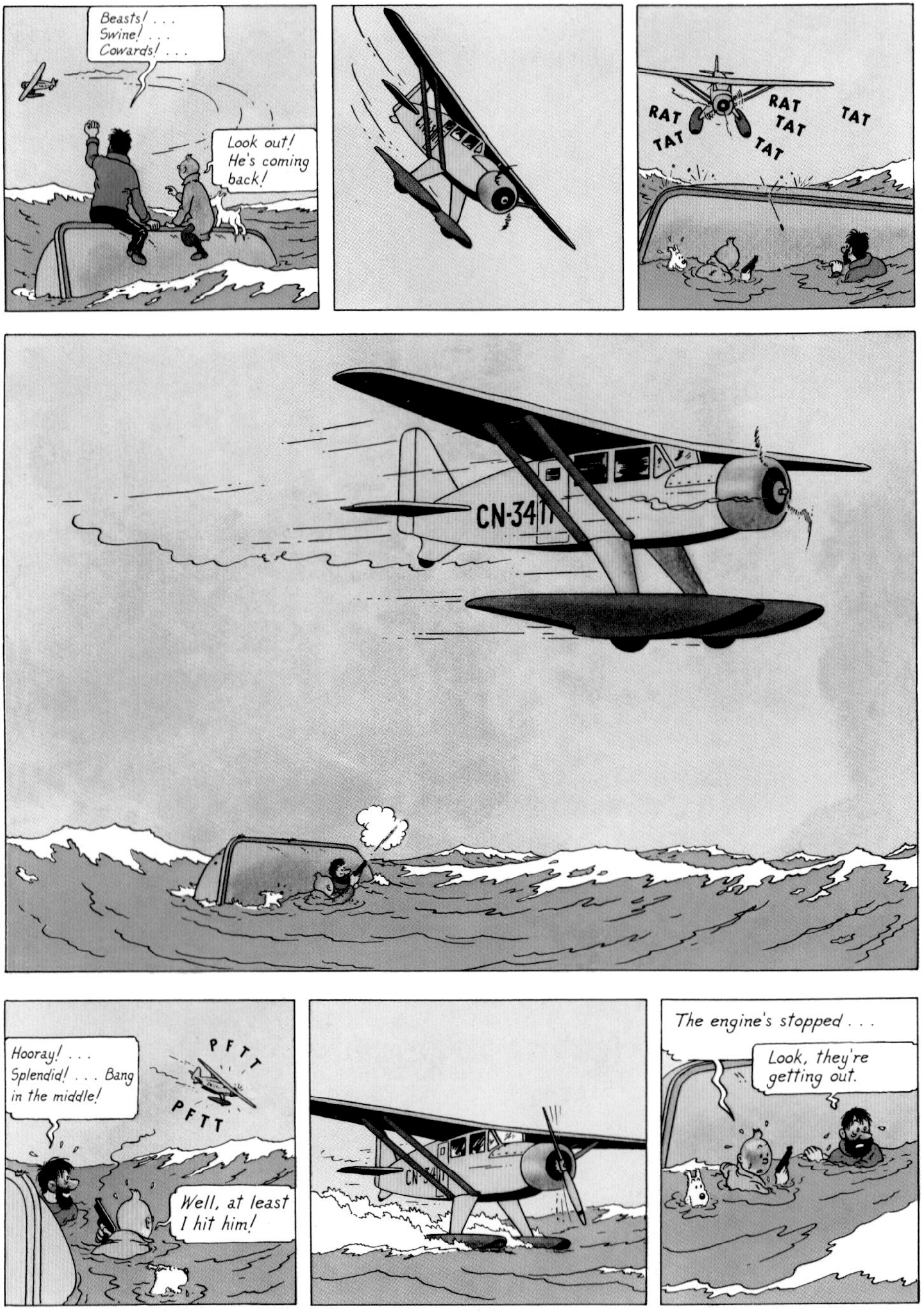
Beasts! . . .
Swine! . . .
Cowards! . . .
Look out! He's coming back!
RAT TAT
RAT TAT TAT
TAT
CN-3411
Hooray! . . . Splendid! . . . Bang in the middle!
PFTT
PFTT
Well, at least I hit him!
The engine's stopped . . .
Look, they're getting out.

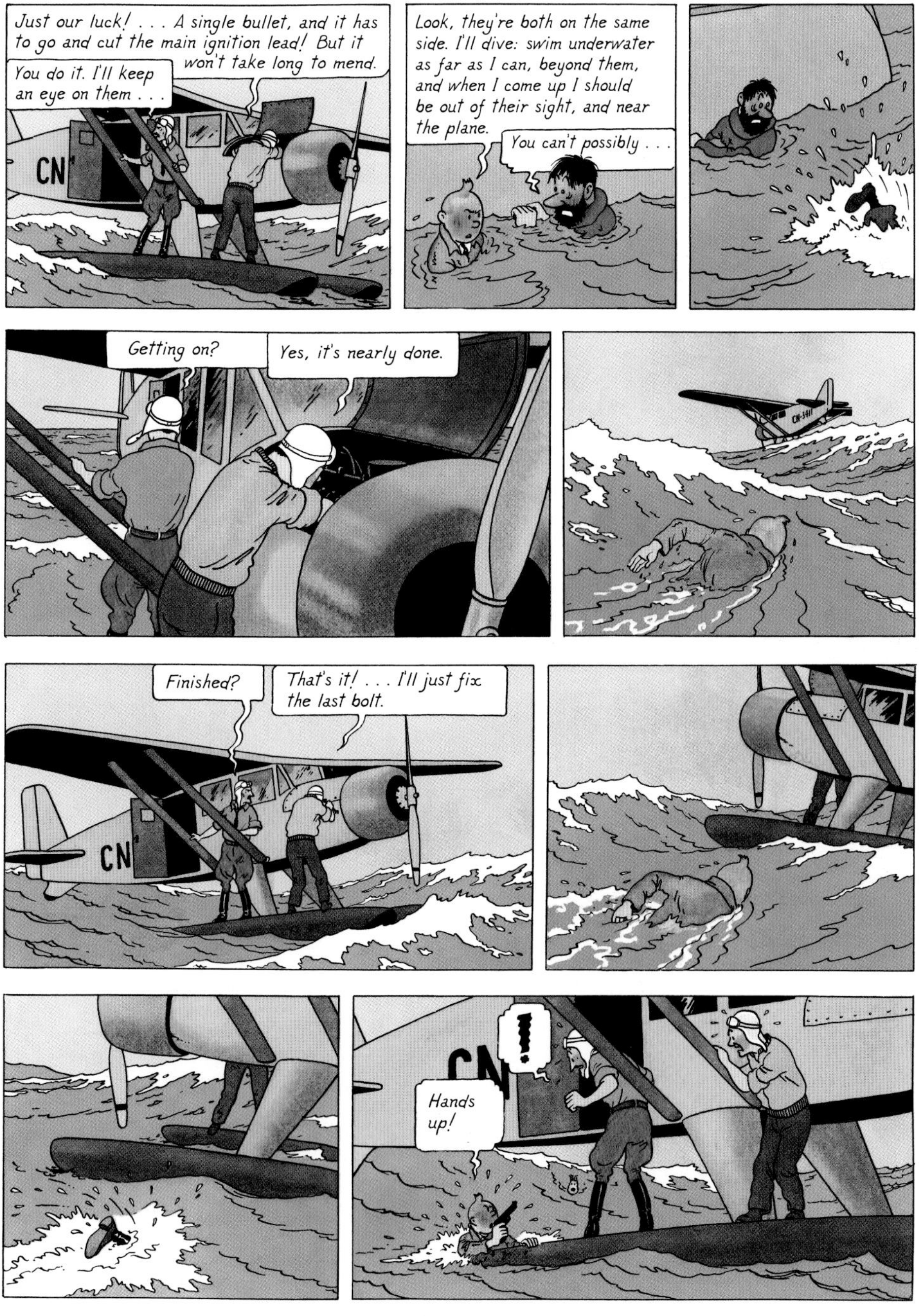
Just our luck! . . . A single bullet, and it has to go and cut the main ignition lead! But it won't take long to mend.
You do it. I'll keep an eye on them . . .
CN
Look, they're both on the same side. I'll dive: swim underwater as far as I can, beyond them, and when I come up I should be out of their sight, and near the plane.
You can't possibly . . .
Getting on?
Yes, it's nearly done.
Finished?
That's it! . . . I'll just fix the last bolt.
CN
CN
Hands up!

Get back . . . and no tricks! I'm a good shot!

He's done it! . . . What a boy! . . .

Good. Try and find some rope to tie up these two toughs.

Tie them up? Why? . . . Let's just pitch them into the sea! They didn't worry about shooting us up, the gangsters!

I know, but we aren't gangsters! . . . Come on, Captain, tie them up and let's get going.

Now then: who hired you two for this shady business?

So! I see why you pretended to be so big-hearted! You wanted to pump us! Well, we aren't talking! . . .

As you like. But perhaps you'll find your tongues when the police get their hands on you.

Hey, can you fly an aeroplane? . . .

You're sure this is the right direction for Spain? . . .   Er . . . yes . . . but it remains to be seen if we'll get there. We're in for a rough time.

Oh, Columbus, this is frightful! . . . We'll never come through alive!

 Oho, a bottle! . . . Now if only it were whisky . . .

 And it is whisky! . . .

 Since we've got to die, I may as well have one last bottle . . .

 Hey, it looks f-f-fun doing that . . . L-l-let me have a go!

This is hardly the moment . . .

 B-b-but I w-w-want to! . . .

Leave that alone! . . .

 Whew, what luck! . . . I just managed to right her . . .

Quick, look behind you!

No good, he can't hear above the engine.

 N-n-now then you whippersnapper! I don't c-c-care for your tricks! . . .

 W-w-will y-you let me t-take over: yes or no? . . . One . . . two . . . three . . .

Leave me alone!

 Then take that, you pig-headed . . .

Great snakes! What happened?

Help! . . . We're going to crash . . .

That was a near thing!

Good heavens! . . . The two prisoners? . . . They're still in the plane . . .

Stop! . . . You're crazy! . . .

Poor Tintin! . . . He's finished . . .

Here . . . take this one! . . .
I'll get the other . . .

Well, here we are! . . . Do you really think this looks like Spain? Er . . . . I . . . anyway it should be . . .

Wooah! Wooah! Wooah!

?

What a bone! . . . Where on earth did you find it?

Come and see! . . . There are lots more . . .

See? . . . Bones for everybody . . .

A camel! . . .

A camel? . . . But there aren't any camels in Spain . . .

Unfortunately we aren't in Spain! . . . We're in the middle of the Sahara Desert!

In the middle of the Sahara! . . . then that animal . . . that animal . . . that animal died of . . . died of . . .

. . . died of thirst, of course!

What's the matter? . . . Feeling faint?

The land of thirst! . . . The land of thirst! . . .

The land of thirst . . .

Courage, Captain, courage! We aren't finished yet.

It looks as if he's at the end of his tether.

The land of thirst . . .

The prisoners have gone!

I see! Their ropes were almost burnt through: it didn't take much to break them.

The land of thirst . . .

Look over there . . . they're too far away now for us to catch them up. Never mind . . .

Come on, Captain! Perhaps we shall be lucky and come across a well!

The land of thirst . . .

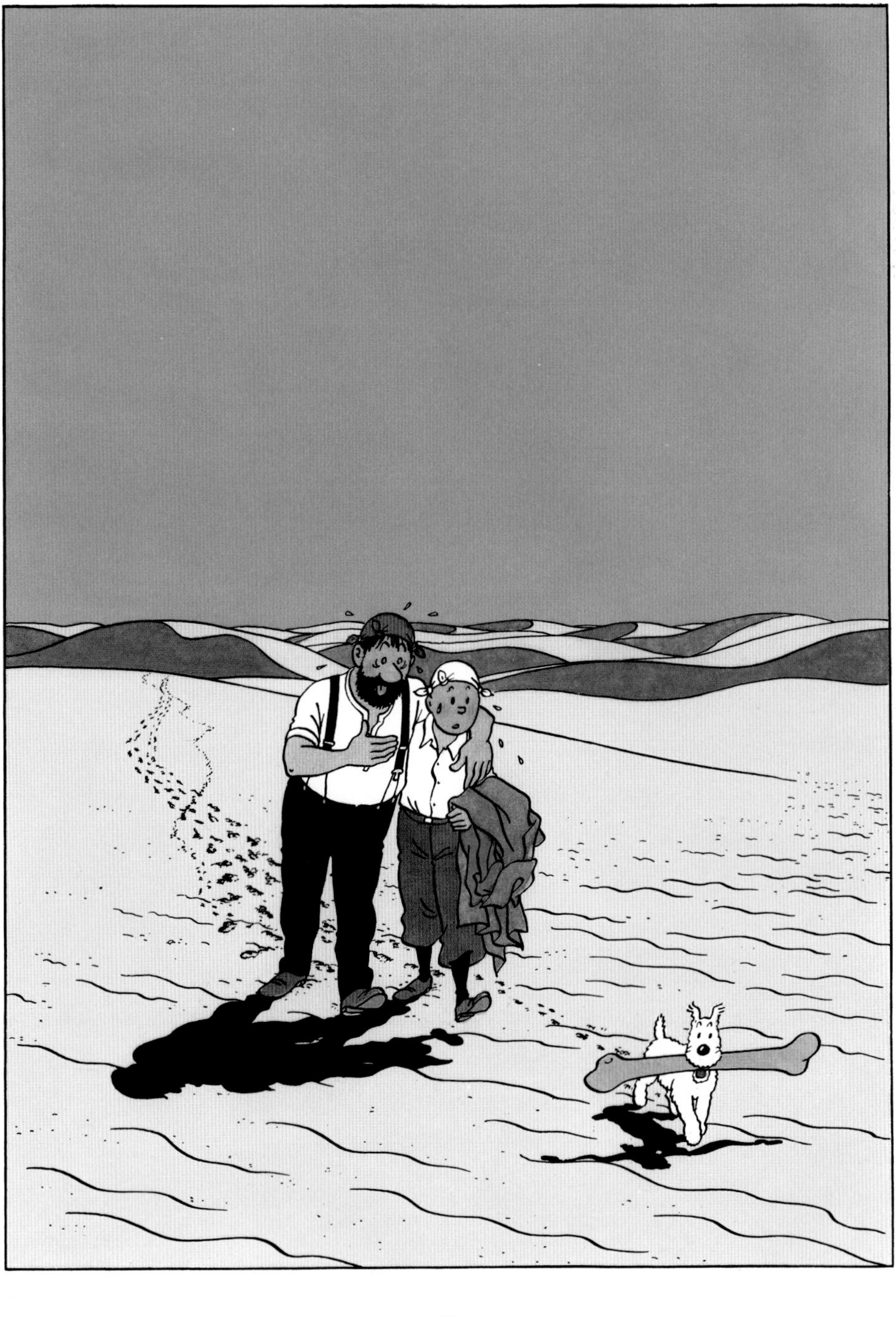

A drink! . . . A drink! . . . I can't go on . . .

Courage, Captain! We'll rest a bit in the shadow of the sand-dune . . .

There, lie down for a while: it'll do you good.

Tintin . . . where are you? . . . A drink! . . .

Just an empty horizon . . . Nothing but endless desert . . .

A drink! . . .

?!*?

I wonder how we can get out of this.

A bottle of champagne! I'll open it!

This confounded cork. It won't come out! . . .

You brute: Take that!

Golly, what have I done?? . . .

160

Thanks all the same, Snowy . . .

I did my best.

We don't want any more of that, please! I'm not a bottle of champagne, so get that into your head!

A drink! . . .

Look! . . . A lake! . . . Water! . . . Water! . . .

?

Stop! Stop! . . . It's a mirage! . . .

Water! . . . Water! . . .

Didn't I tell you it was a mirage? There isn't a lake.

But I saw it . . .

Some hours later . . .

سندلسعب طنتبها دالى...

وسع؟

! مددملالست

Aha! . . . There's a bottle of wine!

Where can he see a bottle?

I'll uncork it . . .

? ? !

BOURG VIEU

I hear you call help?

?!?!

Whew! What a ghastly nightmare!

Where am I? . . . What happened? . . .

You come with me to Lieutenant.

He come, sir . . . the young boy.

Ah! there you are. Come in! I'm glad to see you on your feet again.

I'm Lieutenant Delcourt, in command of the outpost of Afghar.

How do you do, Lieutenant. My name is Tintin. But how . . .

. . . how did you get here? . . . At about midday yesterday my men noticed a column of smoke on the southern horizon. I immediately thought it might be an aeroplane and sent out a patrol. They saw your tracks, found you unconscious, and brought you in.

Oh! Did they find my friend too? . . .

Here he is! . . . Come in, come in. Ahmed, bring three glasses and some drinks . . .

So the smoke was from a plane, then?

Yes, we came down with quite a bump. The machine turned over and caught fire . . .

No thank you. I never drink spirits.

No? . . . Really?

?

Er . . . er . . . no thank you, Lieutenant. I . . . don't either. I . . . I never touch spirits . . .

You don't either? . . . Well, I won't press you.

Anyway, you saved our lives all right, Lieutenant. Without you and your camel patrol we should have died of thirst.

That's why you ought to have a drink with me! . . . But never mind about that. I'd rather you told me what brings you to this forsaken land.

. . . *and here is the latest news. Yesterday's severe gales caused a number of losses to shipping. The steamship TANGANYIKA sank near Vigo, but her crew were all taken off. The merchant vessel JUPITER has been driven ashore, but her crew are safe. An SOS was also picked up from the merchant-ship . . .*

. . . *KARABOUDJAN. Another vessel, the BENARES, went at once to the aid of the KARABOUDJAN and searched all night near the position given in the distress signal. No wreckage and no survivors were found. It must therefore be presumed that the KARABOUDJAN went down with all hands . . .*

That's odd, don't you think?

I should say so! The KARABOUDJAN isn't a cockleshell, to sink without time to launch the boats. It's unbelievable!

That's what I think . . . Lieutenant, is there any way we could leave today? I'm anxious to get to the coast as soon as possible. I'll tell you why.

So soon? . . . Yes, it can be done. It should be enough if I send two guides with you. That area has been quite safe for a couple of months now.

Allah protect them!

Next morning . . .

A wireless message has just come in, sir . . .

Thank you.

MOST URGENT
T.O. 1026 S.C.
Twenty Arab riders reported near Timmin proceeding to Wells of Kefheir. Stop. Dispatch patrol.

By Jupiter! . . . The Wells of Kefheir lie on the route Tintin and his friend are taking! . . .

Ahmed, send my section leaders here at once. And by the way, what did you do with the bottles which were here yesterday?

I not know, sir. I not touch bottles, sir.

Now I'll just have a good swig of this: nobody's watching me.

See! . . . Kefheir . . .

Your very good health, my friends!

CRACK

BANG

BANG

BANG

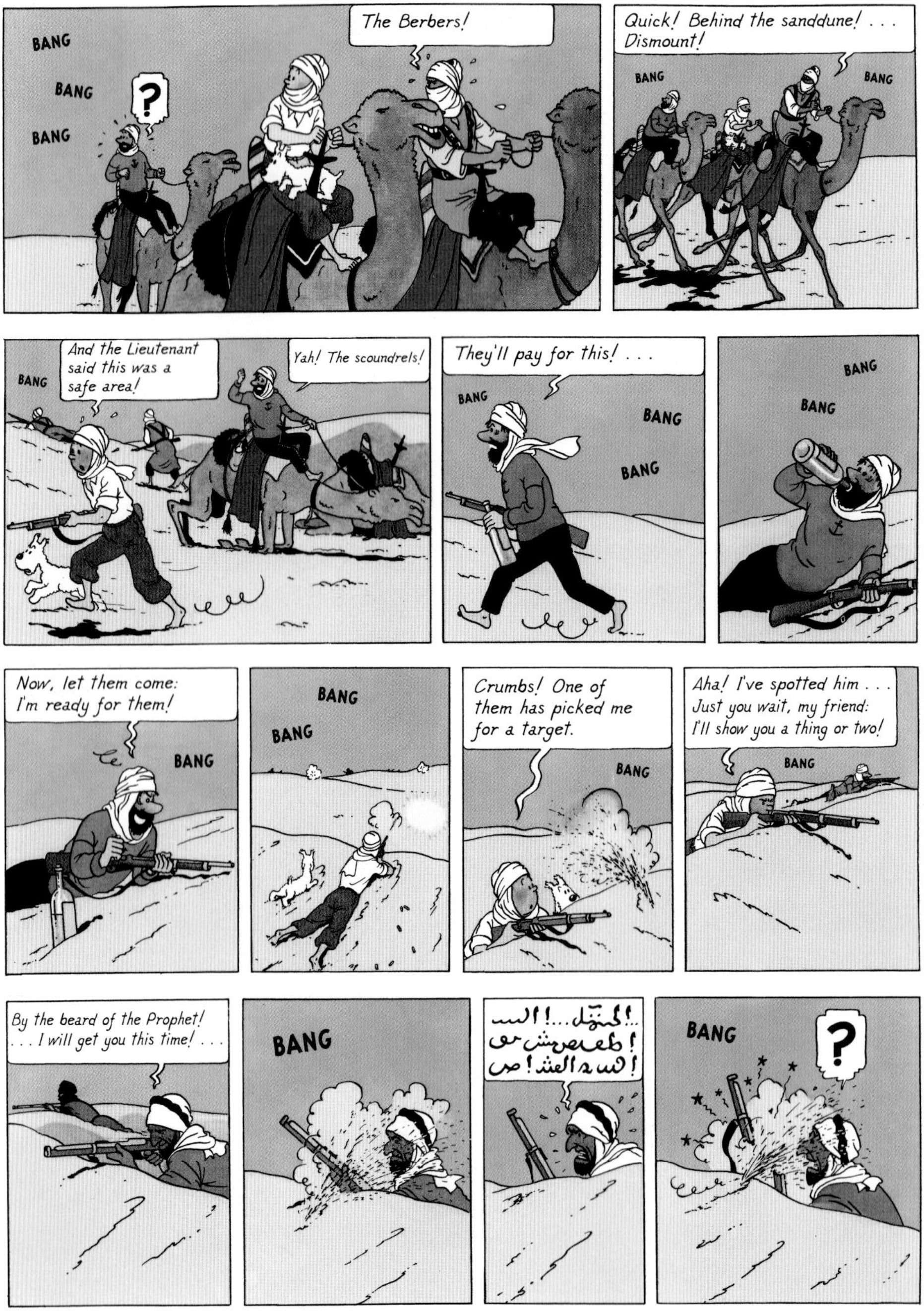

BANG
BANG
BANG
?
The Berbers!
Quick! Behind the sanddune! . . . Dismount!
BANG
BANG
And the Lieutenant said this was a safe area!
BANG
Yah! The scoundrels!
They'll pay for this! . . .
BANG
BANG
BANG
BANG
BANG
Now, let them come: I'm ready for them!
BANG
BANG
BANG
Crumbs! One of them has picked me for a target.
BANG
Aha! I've spotted him . . . Just you wait, my friend: I'll show you a thing or two!
BANG
By the beard of the Prophet! . . . I will get you this time! . . .
BANG
BANG
?

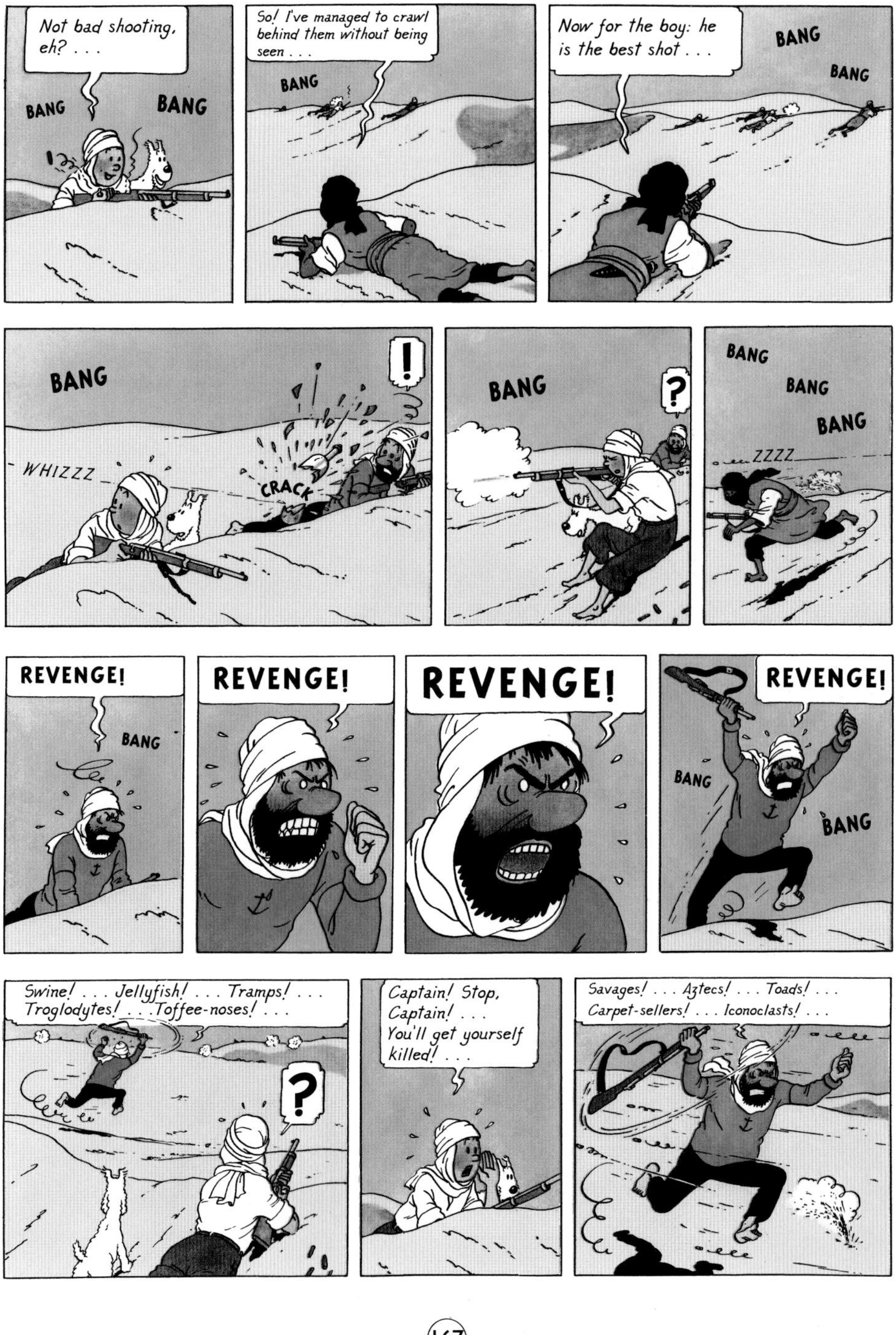
Not bad shooting, eh? . . .
BANG
BANG
So! I've managed to crawl behind them without being seen . . .
BANG
Now for the boy: he is the best shot . . .
BANG
BANG
BANG
!
WHIZZZ
CRACK
BANG
?
BANG
BANG
BANG
ZZZZ
REVENGE!
BANG
REVENGE!
REVENGE!
REVENGE!
BANG
BANG
Swine! . . . Jellyfish! . . . Tramps! . . . Troglodytes! . . . Toffee-noses! . . .
?
Captain! Stop, Captain! . . . You'll get yourself killed! . . .
Savages! . . . Aztecs! . . . Toads! . . . Carpet-sellers! . . . Iconoclasts! . . .

Some saint must watch over drunkards! . . . It's a miracle he hasn't been hit . . .

Rats!... Ectoplasms!... Freshwater swabs!... Bashi-bazouks!... Cannibals!... Caterpillars!...

Cowards! . . . Baboons! . . . Parasites! . . . Pockmarks! . . .

Great snakes! . . . He's got them on the run! . . .

. . . and if you come back you'll feel my rifle-butt! . . .

Well done, Captain! . . . Wonderful! . . .

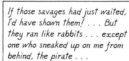

If those savages had just waited, I'd have shown them! . . . But they ran like rabbits . . . except one who sneaked up on me from behind, the pirate . . .

Charge! . . . After them! . . . Take them prisoner! . . .

It's the Lieutenant! . . .

Then . . . then . . . it wasn't me who got rid of those savages . . . it was the Lieutenant . . . ?

We turned up at the right moment, didn't we? . . .

In the nick of time, Lieutenant. But what made you come here?

That's soon explained. This morning I received a radio warning of raiders near Kefheir. We jumped into the saddle right away . . . and here we are! . . .

And now, as soon as my men return with their prisoners we'll all ride north together, to prevent further incidents like this.

After several days' journey, Tintin and the Captain come to Bagghar, a large Moroccan port . . .

First we'll go to the harbour-master. Perhaps he can give us news of the KARABOUDJAN. Good idea . . .

Tintin! . . . Tintin! . . . Where are you going?

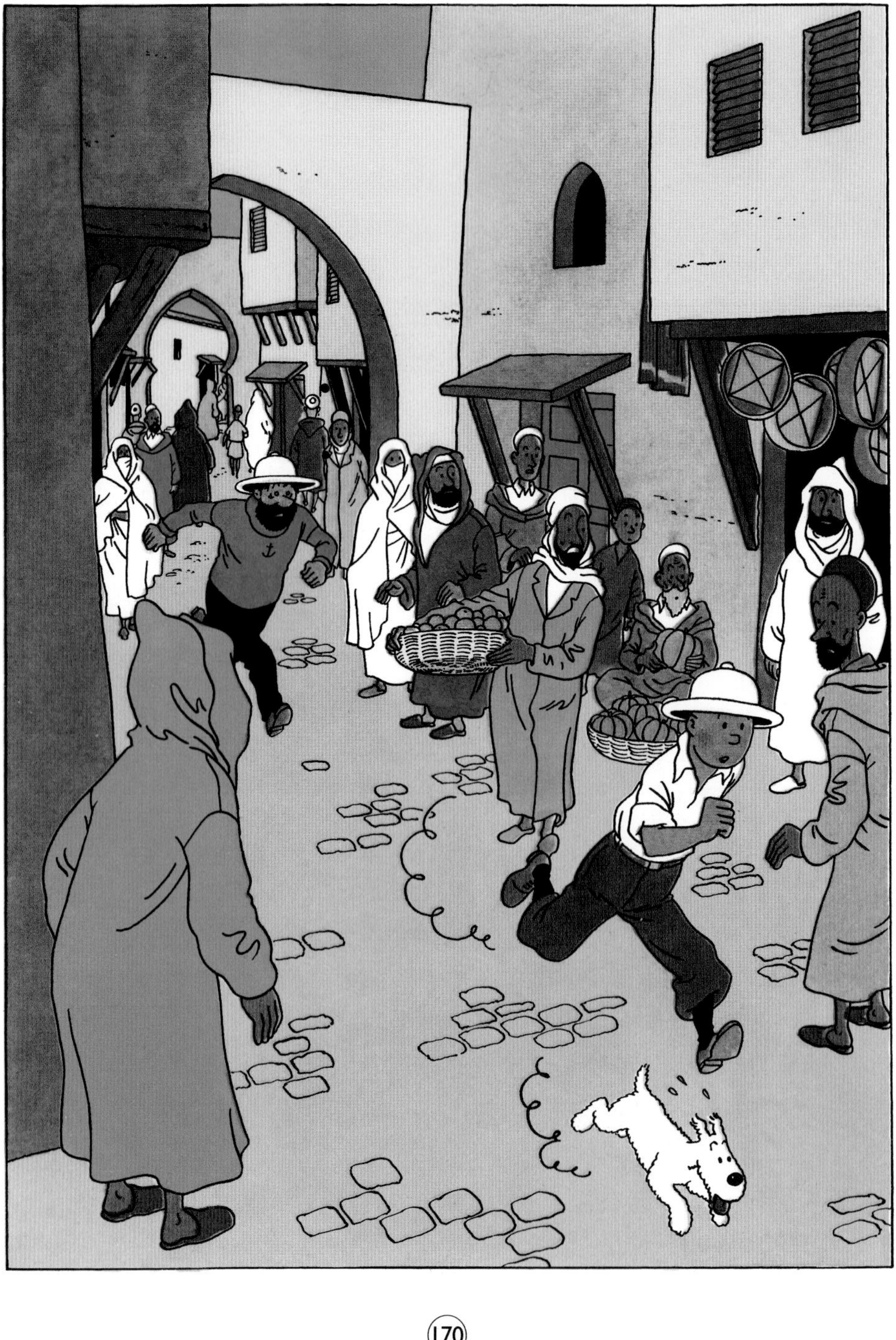

Out of my way, you!

Move along there! Move along!

Bunch of savages! Now I've lost Tintin. What's got into him, I wonder?

Careful! . . . I mustn't lose sight of him.

Now what? . . . He must have gone into one of these houses, but which one? I can't risk being recognised while I wait for him. Never mind: I'll come back.

How shall I ever find Tintin?

The first thing is to find the Captain. I hope he's had the sense to go straight to the harbour-master's office and wait for me there.

And now-now for the h-h-harbour-master! ... H-h-how much, boy?

Five francs.

P-P-POLICE! PO-PO-POLICE!

What's up this time?

I ... I ... it's disgraceful! ... My wallet's been stolen! ... I'll s-s-sue th-them! ... R-r-robbers! ... M-m-my wallet! ...

It's dis-gr-graceful! ... A city of p-p-pick-p-p-pockets ... I w-w-want my wallet! ...

Here's your wallet! ... Stop all that row! ... It had fallen out of your pocket. And don't rouse the whole neighbourhood another time!

!

Now go home! ... If you make any more trouble, we'll run you in. Understand?

OK, a-a-admiral!

Yo-ho ♩♩ and ♪up ♪ she ♩ rises ♫

DJEBEL AMILAH

?

B-b-blistering barnacles! ... that's the K-K-KARABOUDJAN! Police! ... Arrest them! ... Police! ... P-p-police!

P-P-POLICE! PO-POLICE!

I t-t-tell you it's the KARABOUD-BOUD-BOUDJAN, Blistering barnacles! I am ... I am her Captain! ... It's not the DJEBEL-what's it ... You must arrest the l-l-lot of them!

Come along! That's enough!

But I tell you that is the K-K-KARABOUDJAN! ... and she's full of op-opium!

?

The Captain! . . . I must warn the mate at once!

Hello? . . . Yes, it's me . . . What? . . . Are you crazy? . . . You've seen the Captain! . . . Are you sure? He recognised the ship, confound it! . . . He's been arrested . . . OK, I'll come.

Meanwhile . . .

It's funny, he's not come yet. I certainly told him we'd go straight to the harbour-master.

Next morning . . .

Hello . . . Port Control here. Oh, it's you Mr Tintin . . . Captain Haddock? . . . No, we haven't seen him yet.

This is getting me worried. Something must have happened to him. I'd better go to the police.

POLI

Captain Haddock? . . . We've just let him go; he's been gone about five minutes. He was brought in last night for causing a disturbance. When he left he said he was going to the harbour-master's office and he had some very important news for you. If you hurry you'll soon catch him up.

Important news? . . . What can that be?

There he is!

The KARABOUDJAN, here! . . . That will surprise Tintin when I tell him.

Oh! My shoelace has come undone.

HELP!
H.E.L.P!

They've got the Captain!

CRASH

This wretched door won't open! ...

The noise of an engine! ... They must have a car!

Too late!

Another car! ... I'll grab it: I must save the Captain at all costs!

That's got her started! ... Off we go, full speed ahead! ...

What's up? Why are we going backwards? ...

PAAARP! PAAARP! PAAARP!
Stop! The car's horn must have got stuck.

I mustn't let them get away!

Saved! . . . There's a taxi!

Taxi! To the Central Station!

Quick, follow that car!

? ?

Be so good as to get out, young man: I was first.

I beg your pardon, sir, but I was before you!

My dear sir, I am not in the habit of arguing with puppies. Get out! At once! . . . I have to be at the Central Station in fifteen minutes.

And I must get to the hospital urgently . . .

. . . as I've just been bitten by this mad dog!

Quick, driver, follow that car!

Which car, sir?

Which car? . . . Why that one . . . Heavens! It's gone!

Now all I can do is find the alley where I lost the mate of the KARABOUDJAN.

But I ought to wear a burnous to go there, otherwise I might be recognised.

Ah! here's an old clothes shop . . . but . . . but surely . . . I can't be mistaken.

My old friends Thomson and Thompson.

Thank goodness! You're safe and sound. We despaired of ever finding you alive!

I think it's extraordinary, he recognised us at once, in spite of our disguise!

Now tell us: what happened on the KARABOUDJAN? We were amazed when they handed us your wireless signal: 'Have been imprisoned aboard KARABOUDJAN. Am leaving vessel. Cargo includes opium. TINTIN.' We took the first plane for Bagghar . . .

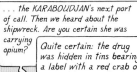

. . . the KARABOUDJAN's next port of call. Then we heard about the shipwreck. Are you certain she was carrying opium?

Quite certain: the drug was hidden in tins bearing a label with a red crab on it, and the words 'EXTRA FINE CRAB'.

Tins of crab? . . . That reminds me . . .

I saw one in the shop where we bought our burnouses just now.

Did you? Quick let's go and see.

It's gone!

What have you done with the tin of crab that was on the table?

It's here, sidi. I put tin here in the cupboard.

That's the one! I recognise the label: it's the same.

Open that tin!

There, sidi . . .

Look!

It's crab!

Of course, sidi, there is crab. Good crab, sidi, best quality . . .

Yes, it's crab all right . . . And yet I saw the same tins aboard the KARABOUDJAN, and they contained opium.

Hmm! . . . Very odd.

To be precise: very odd; in fact, very queer . . .

Tell me: where did you buy this tin?

From Mohammed Ben Ali, sidi; the shop on the corner . . .

Now for Mohammed Ben Ali.

Look!

Hmm, no one about?

To be precise: no one about...

These are the same tins, all right.

Hi! Anybody there!

Hi! Anybody there?

CRASH

BANG

Good gracious! Something's happened to him...

Thomson!... Thomson!... Where are you?

BANG

CRASH

!

All right?

Look out, there's a step.

Nothing broken?

No, all's well.

Yes, all's well.

Mind your hat!...

What are you doing here?

Oh! Are you the owner of this shop?

I would like the name and address of the supplier who sold you the tins of crab you have in your shop.

The tins of crab? They came from Omar Ben Salaad, sidi, the biggest trader in Bagghar. He is very rich, sidi, very very rich . . . He has a magnificent palace, with many horses and cars; he has great estates in the south; he even has a flying machine, sidi, which some people call an aeroplane . . .

Indeed! . . . Thank you very much.

Will you help me, and make discreet inquiries about this Omar Ben Salaad? . . . Among other things, try and find out the registration number of his private plane. But you must be discreet, very discreet.

My friend, you can count on us. We are the soul of discretion. 'Mum's the word', that's our motto.

Yes, that's our motto: 'Dumb's the word' . . .

Now to rescue the Captain. First I must get the right clothes . . .

Hello Mister Mate? . . . This is Tom . . . Yes, we got the Captain. He made a bit of a row but the wharves were deserted and no one heard us . . . What? You'll be along in an hour? . . . OK.

Meanwhile . . .

RUE DE L'OUE

Does Mr Omar Ben Salaad live here? . . . We'd like a word with him.

My master has just gone out, sidi. See, there he is on his donkey . . .

So that's him.

Make way! Make way for the mighty Omar Ben Salaad!

Let's follow him.

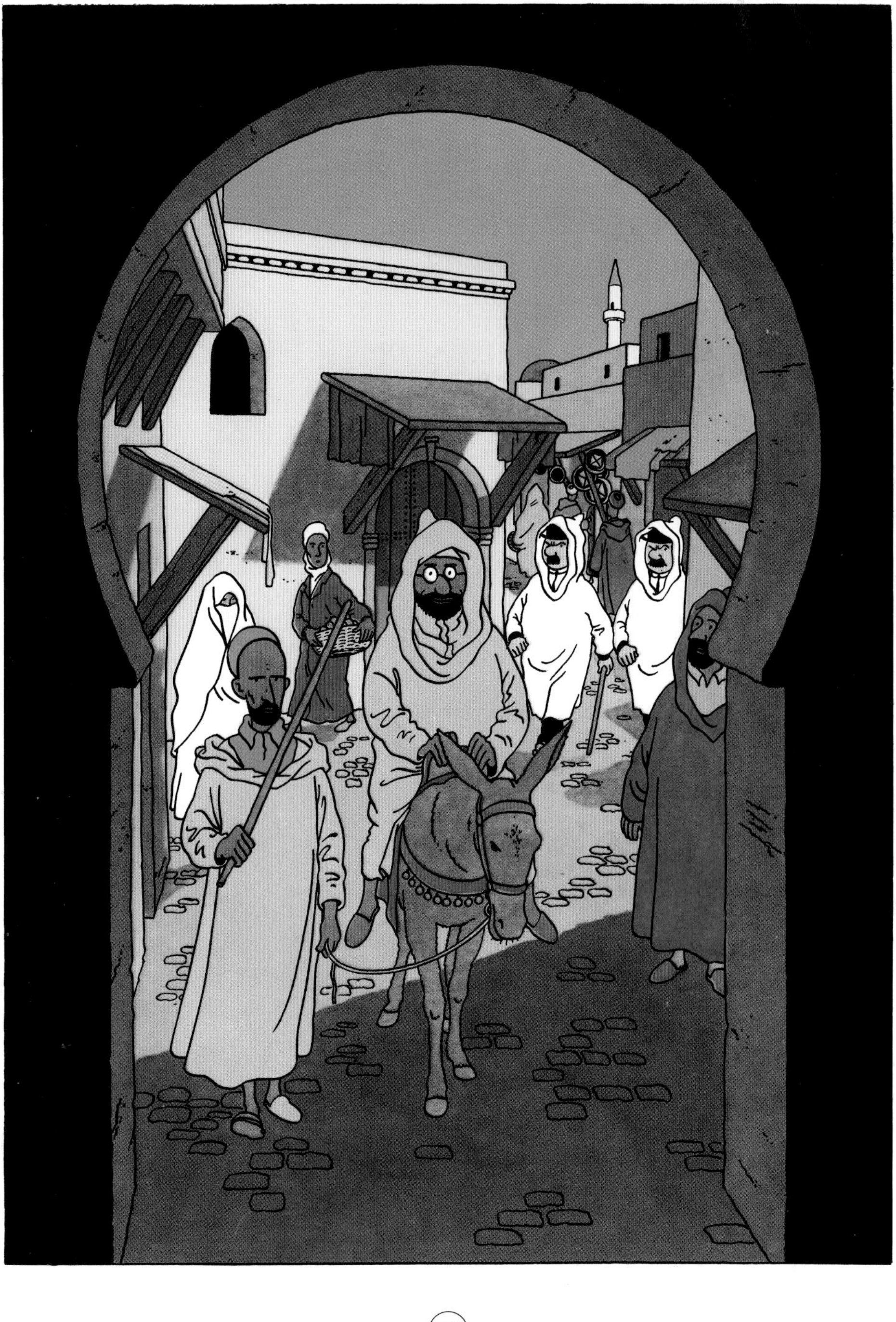

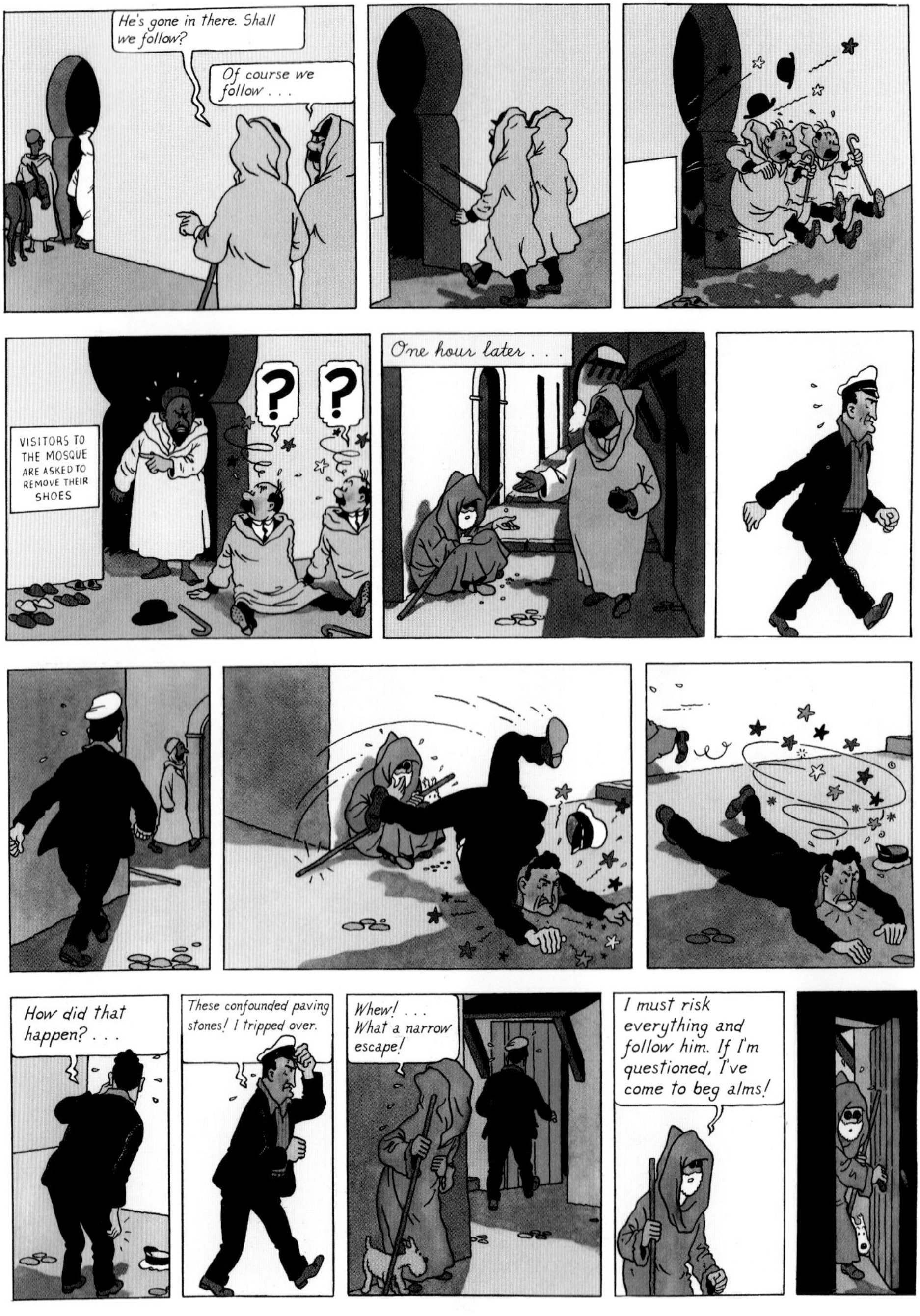

He's gone in there. Shall we follow?
Of course we follow . . .
VISITORS TO THE MOSQUE ARE ASKED TO REMOVE THEIR SHOES
One hour later . . .
How did that happen? . . .
These confounded paving stones! I tripped over.
Whew! . . . What a narrow escape!
I must risk everything and follow him. If I'm questioned, I've come to beg alms!

What do you want here? . . .

Alms, for the love of Allah, the Prophet will reward you . . .

Out you go, verminous beggar! Crawling worm! Begone, son of a mangy dog!

How very polite! . . .

Whew! . . . This is going to be harder than I thought. What next? But where's Snowy, I wonder?

By the beard of the Prophet! . . . Thief!

Come back, you robber! Give me my joint!

Now or never! . . .

A whole joint! . . . Vile dog! If ever I see it again . . . !

Tell me, is Sidi Allan here? . . .

Crumbs! He's back already!

Yes, Abd El Drachm, he has just come.

Quick! . . . I must hide in the cellar.

Good, I'll go to him. Farewell.

Heavens! He's coming down here!

Where's he gone! ... He can't have vanished into thin air! ...

No secret passage, and no trap-door; the walls and floor sound absolutely solid. It must be magic.

WOOAH!

Snowy! ... You frightened the life out of me!

You rascal, now I see. You hid in the ventilator shaft to eat that joint!

As for me, Snowy, I'm like old Diogenes, seeking a man! You've never heard of Diogenes! ... He was a philosopher in ancient Greece, and he lived in a barrel ...

Lived in a barrel! ... In a barrel, Snowy! ... Great snakes! I think I've got it!

Let's see if this barrel will open ...

And it does! There are hinges here!

Look Snowy ... A way out!

And a door the other end! We're certainly on the right track, Snowy ...

Hooray! The tins of crab from the KARABOUDJAN.

BANDITS!

BRUTES!

That's the Captain's voice! . . .

Yell as loud as you like; no one can hear you. Now why not be sensible? For the last time: where is Tintin?

HERE! . . .

Hand's up! . . . No one move! You there, untie the Captain . . .

Give me your hand, Tintin! . . . Give me your hand! . . .

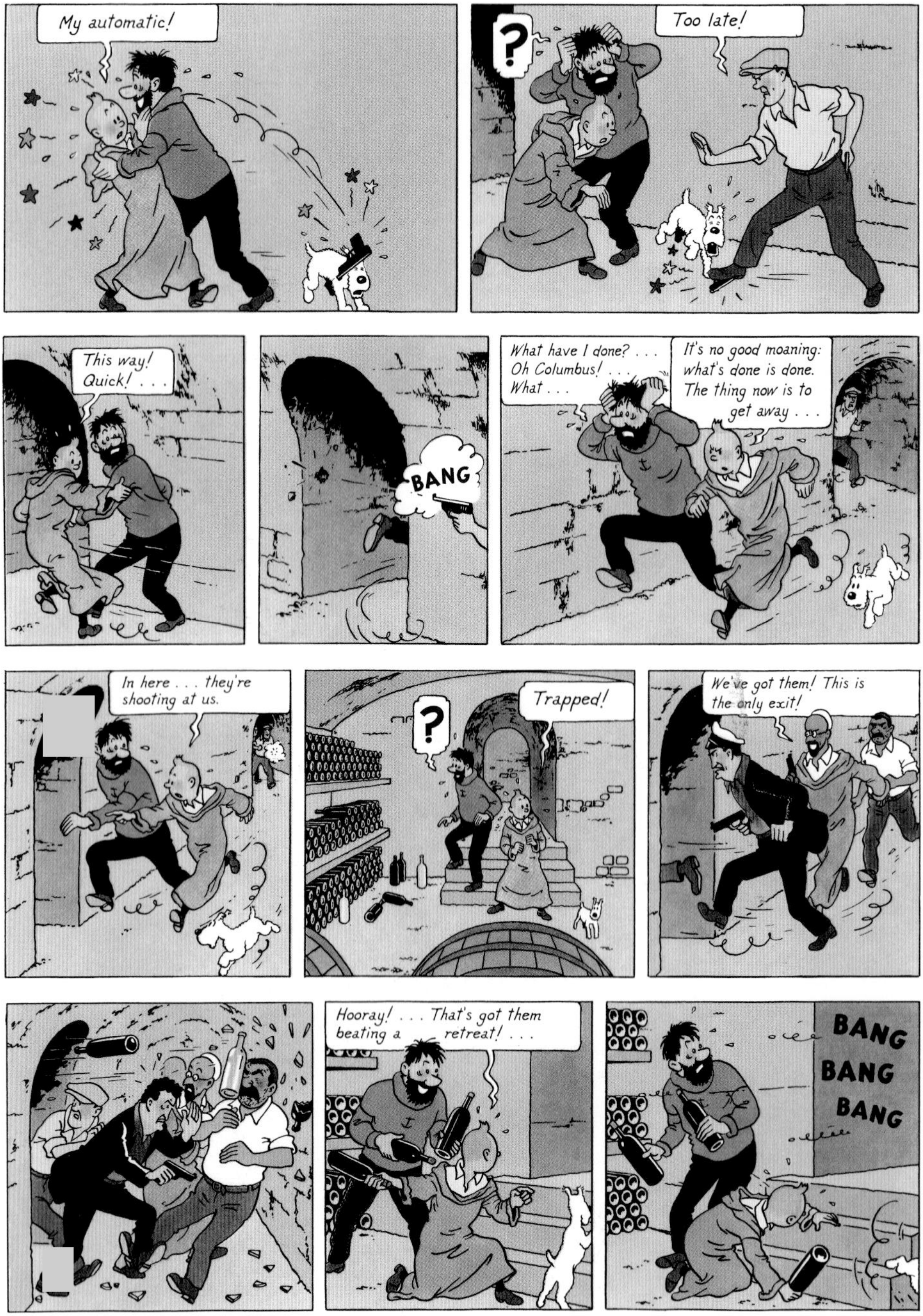
My automatic!
Too late!
?
This way! Quick! . . .
BANG
What have I done? . . . Oh Columbus! . . . What . . .
It's no good moaning: what's done is done. The thing now is to get away . . .
In here . . . they're shooting at us.
?
Trapped!
We've got them! This is the only exit!
Hooray! . . . That's got them beating a retreat! . . .
BANG
BANG
BANG

Ooooh! All that wine! ... What a terrible waste! ...

Now then, no nonsense! ... This isn't the time for drinking!

What do you take me for? A drunkard?

What's happening! ... My head's reeling ...

I'm the king of the castle ♪

They're tight!

Ta - ra - ra - ♫ boom - de - ay ♪ ♫

For tonight we'll merry ♫ merry be, for tonight we'll merry merry be ... ♪

Yes, they're drunk: the fumes from the wine, I suppose. Now we can just go in and get them.

Ta - ra - ra ♫ boom ... ♪

We'll take this one. You bring the other.

Tiddley - om - pom - ♫ pom ... ♪

I'm the king of the caaa- ♫ -aastle ...

That's enough! Let go of that bottle! ...

You bully! My bottle! ... Treason! ... Revenge! ... Twister! ... Heretic! ... Slave-trader! ... Technocrat!

Buccaneer! Vegetarian! Politician!

If he makes trouble I'll soon settle his hash!

Pirate! . . . Corsair!

Quiet, you drunken old fool! . . .

HARLEQUIN!

HYDROCARBON!

ABORIGINE!

POLYNESIAN! GYROSCOPE!

?!

Revenge!

Blackamoor! . . . Anthracite! . . . Coconut! . . . Fuzzy-wuzzy! . . . Cannibal! . . .

Go on! Seek! Seek! Bite him!

Athropithecus! . . . Blackbird! . . .

Tiddley - om - pom - pom ♫

Meanwhile . . .

See, the great Omar Ben Salaad has returned from the mosque.

Shall we go and ask him a few questions?

Good idea!

Master, two strangers are here and would speak with you. They say they are making some inquiries.

Good. Show them in; I will see them.

Mr Omar, we have been asked to carry out an investigation . . .

A discreet investigation, of course . . .

Oh? . . . And what is the object of your investigation?

A young friend of ours, called Tintin, suspects that you are concerned in drug-running.

Are you, Mr Salaad?

?!

By the beard of the Prophet! . . . Who dares suspect Omar Ben Salaad? . . . Get out, infidel dogs! Get out, or I'll have you flogged to death!

?

Nincom-poop!

Anacoluthon! . . . Invertebrate! . . . Liquorice!

Tintin!!

?

Seek! Seek!

So, you are Tintin! Well, this time my young friend your last hour has come!

Careful now, careful! It's dangerous to play with firearms . . .

?

BANG

سب !!

Who is this man?

Omar Ben Salaad! We have just questioned him, and he assured us he is absolutely innocent . . .

What a weight!

Him, innocent? . . . I've just found tins of opium in his cellar . . . And look . . .

Look at this! Two crab's claws, made of gold. He's the ringleader. I'm certain. Quick, telephone the police!

Hello, hello, police? This is Thomson and Thompson, certified detectives. After a long and dangerous investigation we have succeeded in unmasking a gang of opium smugglers . . . Yes, exactly . . . and their leader is a man by the name of Ben Salaad. We have him at your disposal.

What did you say? . . . Omar Ben Salaad? . . . Are you pulling my leg? Omar Ben Salaad, the most respected man in all Bagghar, and you've . . .

. . . caught him, yes! . . . And if that's not the truth may the heavens fall!

Quite right!

Omar Ben Salaad an opium smuggler! Well, that beats everything! But . . . what's going on now? . . .

Swine! . . . Vampire! . . .

It's him again!

Hooray! The police! . . .

Arrest that man! . . . He's a gangster, p-p-pirate . . . He . . . he . . . he beat me with a st-stick . . .

It's not a stick you need, it's a wallop with my truncheon!

At last, the police! . . . Gentlemen, this is the man we have brought to justice.

To be precise: . . . this is the man!

Some of your men come with me: there are more of them in the cellar!

The mate has escaped: and he's the most dangerous of the lot . . .

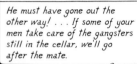

He must have gone out the other way! . . . If some of your men take care of the gangsters still in the cellar, we'll go after the mate.

We'll go down to the harbour. He's a sailor, so he'll probably make for there . . .

? Police! Police!

Someone's stolen one of the motorboats I look after! A man jumped aboard and he was gone in a flash!

There he is! It's him! Quick, another boat!

Hey, she won't go!

The painter! . . . You've forgotten to slip the painter!

Of course, we've forgotten the painter!

Wait: I've got a knife. It's quicker!

All right?

That's it!

We're overhauling him! . . . Our boat is faster than his!

By thunder! They're after me!

Confound it! ... The engine's stalled! ... Crumbs! Where are Thomson and Thompson?

Something's fouled the propeller ...

A fishing net! ... Fine! Off we go again ...

Devil take him: He's on my tail again! ...

Take that! ...

... and that! ...

... and that! ...

The boat's lurching wildly! ... What a fight! ... Ah! One of them's getting up ... Who? ...

It's Tintin! ... He's got the best of it! ... He's swinging round, and coming back! ...

Quick! Give me that telescope!

?!

Hooray! He's got the mate!
... So that's the lot from the KARABOUD-JAN! ...

Steady on, Sergeant! ... None of that! ... Thanks to Captain Haddock we've arrested the DJEBEL AMILAH, which is none other than the camouflaged KARABOUDJAN, and rounded up the crew ...

Quickly! There's someone waiting for you up there.

Heartiest congratulations, Mr Tintin!

?

Who is this chap?

Allow me to introduce myself: Bunji Kuraki of the Yokohama police force. The police have just freed me from the hold of the KARABOUDJAN where I was imprisoned. I was kidnapped just as I was bringing you a letter ...

Oh! So it was you ...

Yes, I wanted to warn you of the risk you were running. I was on the track of this powerful, well-organised gang, which operates even in the Far East. One night I met a sailor called Herbert Dawes ...

... who was one of my crew ...

... and later was drowned ...

That's it. He was drunk, and boasted that he could get me some opium. To prove it he showed me an empty tin, which, he said, had contained the drug. I asked him to bring me a full tin the next day. But next day he did not come and I was kidnapped ...

And they must have done away with him: but why was a bit of a label found on him, with the word KARABOUDJAN, in pencil?

Well, I asked him the name of his ship. He was so drunk I couldn't hear what he mumbled. So he wrote it on a scrap of the label, but then he put the paper in his own pocket ...

Some days later...

... and it is thanks to the young reporter, Tintin, that the entire organisation of the Crab with the Golden Claws today find themselves behind bars.

This is the Home Service. You are about to hear a talk given by Mr Haddock, himself a sea-captain, on the subject of ...

... drink, the sailor's worst enemy.

RRRING

Good-morning, Mr Tintin . . . Your letters . . . and a parcel . . .

What's in this parcel?

Why not open it?

I don't trust this! . . . It might be a bomb! Those gangsters are capable of anything . . .

To Snowy, from an admirer

Now, let's listen to the Captain . . .

. . . for the sailor's worst enemy is not the raging storm; it is not the foaming wave . . .

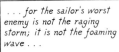

. . . which pounds upon the bridge sweeping all before it; it is not the treacherous reef lurking beneath the sea, ready to rend the keel asunder; the sailor's worst enemy is drink!

Phew! . . . How hot these studios are! . . .

GLUG GLUG GLUG . . . . CRASH . . . . ZZING . . . . BRR . . . .

What's happening?

This is the Home Service. We must apologise to our listeners for this break in transmission, but Captain Haddock has been taken ill . . .

Hello, Broadcasting House? This is Tintin. Have you any news of Captain Haddock? I hope it's nothing serious . . .

No, nothing serious. The Captain is much better already . . . Yes . . . No . . . He was taken ill after drinking a glass of water . . .

THE END

HERGÉ-